MW01611612

HEADER

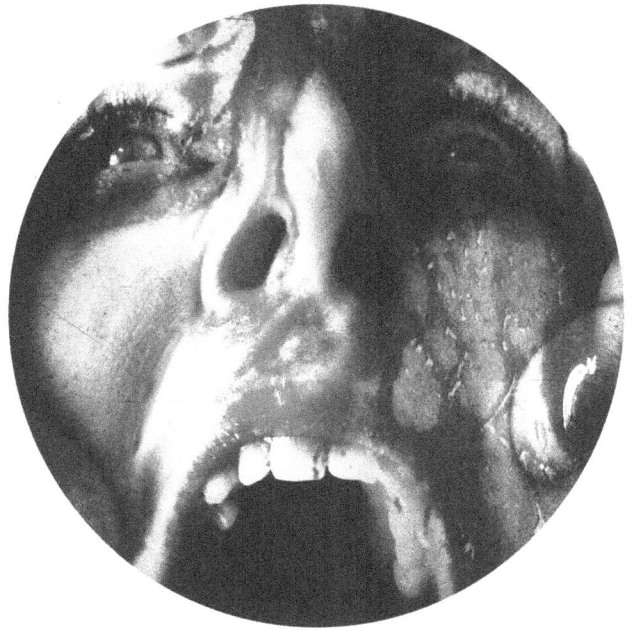

EDWARD LEE

deadite
press

DEADITE PRESS
205 NE BRYANT
PORTLAND, OR 97211
www.DEADITEPRESS.com

AN ERASERHEAD PRESS COMPANY
www.ERASERHEADPRESS.com

ISBN: 1-62105-061-0

Copyright © 2012 HEADER, LLC
www.whatsaheader.com

Cover art copyright © 2012 Stephen Romano
www.shockfestival.net

Printed in the USA.

*Dedicated in loving memory of Dick Mullaney,
We'll miss you Grandpappy.*

1924—2010

ON HEADER, NEEDLEPOINT, AND THE JOURNAL OF AMERICAN MEDICINE BY JACK KETCHUM

What's a header?

If you don't know by now I'm not going to be the one to tell you. I'll tell you what it isn't, though.

Baseball terminology. Double or triple.

A conundrum or tricky problem.

The opposite of a footer.

Okay, I take it back. I *will* tell you what it is. Sort of.

A header is something created by Edward Lee, which to my knowledge had never been dreamt of before it entered his own fevered brain to do so. I can almost see him at the time gleefully relishing the fact that he'd come up with—if not an entirely new word—certainly a brand-new usage. Which I am morally certain will one day wind up in Wikipedia. Perhaps the re-release of this novella, along with the dandy little film based upon it, will hasten that inevitability.

Glee is a hallmark of both Lee's life and work anyway. When I picture Lee, I most always picture him smiling. That smile has a lot of mischief in it but also simple joie de vivre. Give him an ice cold beer, a seat at an outdoor café where he can watch The Girls of Summer go by, and he's one happy camper. Give him good conversation and the smile will invariably appear at some point no matter how serious the subject matter. It says *life is good.*

I've seen that smile most memorably on two occasions. The first was at some long-ago World Horror Convention in Nashville—our first, Lee's and mine—when having retreated back to our hotel room for a breather and a stiff drink it became perfectly clear to us pair of hermit writers that not only were a lot of these horror people happy to meet us, they'd been *waiting* to meet us. That they knew and really liked our work. That astonishingly, some of the people *we'd* been reading and whose work we admired also admired us.

We had us a kind of Cinderella moment here.

I remember Lee pacing the room beer bottle in one hand and cigarette in the other. shaking his head and grinning.

The second occasion was slightly more recent.

In 2003 the pair of bold and utterly self-destructive lunatics who decided *Header* would make a great movie—Michaels Kennedy and Anthony—also decided it would be cool to have Lee and his good buddy Ketchum do walk-ons as a pair of cops who find a nude dead body along the side of the road. Never mind that Lee had never acted before and though I had, it was one hellova long time ago. Naturally we jumped at the idea. If nothing else—me living in New York and Lee in Florida—it was an excuse to have a few drinks together.

And then there was that nude dead body.

So next thing you know, a production assistant is driving us from Buffalo airport up into the hills above the sleepy little town of Ellicotville, New York. Our scene isn't until tomorrow but we're going to watch the shoot. We pull off onto a dirt road. It had rained the night before so it's actually a mud road. Pretty dismal day. Cold for this time of year. We drive a little while and then there ahead of us is this wooden shack out in the middle of nowhere. The door has a pair of antlers on it.

This is Grandpap's shack.

Wow says Lee or something like that. He's a little wide-eyed.

We get out and are greeted warmly by director Archie and his crew and by Elliot Kotek, who plays Travis.

They're shooting interiors today so we step over cables

and equipment through the doorway and there's Dick Mullaney, who plays Grandpap, sitting in his wheelchair with the makeup woman working quietly on his bloody wound. In front of him is his old battered worktable. Shoes and shoe-molds and more antlers and tools and clutter all over the place. And this is when the second smile appears.

This is great! says Lee or something like that. *This is perfect! This is just the way I imagined it!*

He shakes hands with Mullaney. You're *perfect too!* he says.

Another Cinderella moment. And I don't think I've seen that kind of delight on someone's face who *wasn't* five years old before or since.

Though maybe if I'd had a mirror at my first day of shooting on *The Lost* I'd have seen it on my own. It's possible.

The point to all this is that to some—though not all—of us writers glee comes quite naturally and quite frequently. We're aware that what we're doing here is play. High-level play that paradoxically we've worked very hard to come by but play all the same. We have a lot of fun at this. Think of Kathleen Turner in the beginning of *The Jewel of the Nile* as she finishes typing the last few lines of her western romance novel, tears streaming down her face, laughing and sobbing in sheer joy. To writers especially it's funny as hell.

Because it's exactly like that sometimes.

Life is good.

It's almost as good when a bunch of talented, energetic people are working to re-create what you've done in another medium. They're playing too. The only difference is, the game they're all playing was put in motion by you. When it works it's pretty damn gratifying on many levels.

But it's really a lot like having somebody reading you too.

Reading's play, isn't it?

I don't care if you're reading J. K. Rowling or James

7

Joyce, a how-to on needlepoint or The Journal of American Medicine. The game this time is to get into the writer's head, see things from his or her point of view, take it in and make it part of you, at least for a little while.

You? You're about to take in *Header*. I wish you well.

It is a rough and funny game.

Lee made it that way.

Gleefully.

Header.

Havin' a header tonight, we is!

We'se gonna have ourselfs a header so fierce ol' Tully Natter'll be shittin' in his grave!

He'd heard the term, in all its variations so many times, but he just couldn't figure it.

Header.

What *was* it?

The little boy's eyes widened in the dark, blooming like nightflowers. He hid in the closet, a crouched and frozen shadow; he cracked the door half an inch, but he couldn't quite see them. His curiosity burned.

He had to know, he *had* to know what this thing was they were doing.

He'd heard them speak of it many times—only, though, in the least-formed whispers, behind the slickest grins and eyes narrowed to forbidden slits. Yes, Daddy and his grandfather, and sometimes Uncle Helton. Like just today, when Daddy had brought his tractor in from the graze field.

"That blammed Caudill up an' cut my fence," Daddy'd railed. Grandpap looked up from his work table. "Agin?"

"Yeah, shore's shit! Lost six more sheep! Gawd Almighty, we'se gonna have to *do* somethin' 'bout this!"

And that's when Grandpap had smiled that feisty, whiskery smile of his. "What we'se gonna have to do, son, is have ourselfs a header."

"Dag straight! Fucker stole my sheep, third time this year. Tonight, we'se gonna have a header fer shore! Teach that cracker som-bitch ta steal *my* sheep!"

See, that's what they'se always called it—whatever *it* was. A header.

Like one time he'd overheard his Daddy whispering to Grandpap, whispers like creaky, tiny etchings. "McCraw burned down one'a Meyers' grain sheds, Pap. He's havin' a header tonight, wants us ta join in." So later on, they'd corn-liquored up and left, and they didn't return till almost dawn.

The little boy couldn't imagine what a header could be, but he knew this: next day at school, Jannie McCraw wasn't in class, and she was never seen again . . .

* * *

"Sweetheart?" Cummings leaned over the bed, gently nudged his girlfriend's warm shoulder. *Christ,* he thought. Bleary morning light seeped in through the window; starlings chirped. Groggily, then, Kath looked up and smiled.

Special Agent Stewart Cummings smiled back. *My love,* he thought. What would he do without her? And this—*this*—crushed him. To see her so sick all the time, so despondent. She deserved better than this, for sure. *And what am I doing to make her life better?* Cummings dared to ask himself. At the very least, he was doing the best he could.

But that wasn't good enough.

She was always so pale, always sniffling. The dark circles under her eyes, like smudges of charcoal, only reinforced her turmoil. *What would I do without her?* She'd come through for him, hadn't she? Waiting tables at the Village Pump while he finished his degree. Now she was sick, and it was his turn to pay her back.

But it was so . . . hard.

"Be careful at work, honey," she peeped to him, so loving, so real.

"Where's your prescription?" Cummings asked. "I'll pick it up on the way home tonight."

"No, no," she insisted amid the sheets. "I'll get it later. I just need a little time to get going, you know."

"Sure, Kath."

"And you work so hard, I'd feel terrible if you had to drive all the way into town just for my medicine."

"Honey, it's no troub—"

"Hush!" she insisted, sniffling once more. Some kind of walking pneumonia, the doctor's slip had said. She'd been like this for months now. "You go on. You do enough for me. I'll get my medicine later."

Cummings kissed her full, pink lips. He wanted to cry.

He left the house, got into his unmarked car, and started

it up. The light of dawn seemed like the color of misery. *Poor Kath,* he thought. Would she ever get better?

And another question rose, with the same heat as the sun.

Her medication cost $450 per month. Not to mention the mortgage, the power bill, groceries.

What would his father say, if he knew what he was doing?

Shit, Cummings thought and drove off.

* * *

Header.

Grandpap, what's a . . . header? Travis recalled askin' just after his 16th birthday. The day before, n'fact, he'd got up an' busted fer hot-wirin' Cage George's '74 Hemi 'Cuda, drunk on shine, and wreckin' it with that cute li'l Kari Ann Wells sitting right next ta him, strokin' his bone an' eventually poppin' a good, hot creamer right in her purdy face. Bone, see, was what they called a fella's dick in these parts, but quad was what they called Kari Ann Wells after that wreck. Weren't Travis' fault she'd broked her blammed back when he droved inta that bridge 'buttment. But 'fore that, Travis had heard about headers many times, heard his daddy talkin' 'bout it with Grandpap, but they was just the tiniest whispers, see, so tiny Travis never learnt really what it was. And ol' Grandpap Martin, later on that same fine day, while's sewin' up a new pair of workboots an' sipping some shine hisself, had answered, *Cain't be tellin' ya that, son, not till ya got some hair 'tween yer legs.*

Travis figured this was Grandpap's way of suggestin' that he was too young to hear such things, an' never mind that he already had a good plot of hair 'tween his legs and could squirt a man-sized nut any ol' time. But what miffed Travis most was this: if he were too young ta hear about headers, how come the blammed county prosser-cueter hadn't felt he was too young to be tried as a ay-dult? *It's 'cos yer hillfolk, boy, yer creek people,* Grandpap had attempted to explain on sentencing day. The fine old man had tears in his eyes sayin' it. *Ain't no one round here cares 'bout hillfolk. All a*

13

bunch of dirty redneck crackers tryin' ta act like fancified city folk, they is. Ya gots ta do yer time now, boy, and ya gots to be good while yer in the blammed stone motel, otherwise they'll se keep ya longer.

Longer? Chrast. That fancified queer-loving judge had dropped *five years* on poor Travis' head.

But, shore enough, Grandpap had been right. Those five years he'd gotten fer the candyass GTA had turned ta eleven a mite quick. Russell County Detent weren't no picnic, and havin' ta beat the livin' shit outa fellas piled those extra years on faster'n shit through one 'a Dumar McGern's chickens. Travis ain't had no choice, 'less he wanted to get butt-fucked ever night and have a bunch of big, dirty fellas callin' him "baby." He'd *busted* some heads, he did, spent a lot of time in the hole fer it—BEV SEG, they called it, though, fer Behavioral Segregation, whatever in tarnation that meant—and then there was that one night when some fella from Crick City doin' a pound for armed robbery had held a prison shiv to Travis' throat and dropped his drawers. "Suck it, cracker, and suck it good. Suck it like you suck yer daddy, 'cos everbody knows all you crackers are queer," this fella ordered. "Suck out that nut, cracker. Be the best meal ya had since the last time the chow hall served cream a' broccoli soup. Make yer daddy jealous, sugar." Well, fer one, Travis' daddy was dead, and he didn't much like ta hear talk like that, and two, there weren't no way in Hade's Place that Travis Clyde Tuckton was gonna suck dick—*gettin'* sucked, shore, but doin' the suckin' hisself? No way, uh-uh! So he snapped that shiv right outa that fella's hand and poked him good in the eye. Stuff came out that looked like the cranberry marmalade they sold down at Hull's General Store. Didn't matter much *what* it looked like, though. Just added more time to Travis' hitch.

But now he was back. And, havin' no place ta go—while he were in stir, the house that his daddy'd left him were hit by lightnin' and burnt down—so's he tromped straight ta Grandpap Martin's neat little clapboard cottage out in the woods.

14

"Travis Clyde Tuckton!" Grandpap had about fuckin' rejoiced upon seein' Travis' big shuck-an'-jive grinnin' mug.

"Hey Grandpap." Travis' eyes, though, held to the rotting wood floor. "I got's ta admit, I feel like a right horse's bee-hind comin' straight here right after I get out the county detent." Travis felt ashamed. "Got no job, no green, nothin' goin' fer me. Shee-it, Grandpap. I'se a *loser.*"

Grandpap's old whiskery face turned stern. Same way his daddy's face turned that time he'd caught Travis stickin' his bone into one'a the sheep. *Dammit, Travis!* Daddy had yelled. *Ya poop out yer brains the last time ya took a shit!? Chrast, boy! Ya wanna hump a sheep, ya nevah hump yer own sheep, dumbass! Ya sneak over ta Caudill's field and hump his sheep!* And then Daddy'd given him a whuppin' like he'd never forgot, but Travis figured he deserved it. And, anyways, that's what Grandpap's face looked like right now.

"Travis, I don't wants ta hear no talk like that *evah!* Yore blood, boy, from my only daughter's loins, and yous are always welcome in my house. An' don't'cha be down-talkin' yerself fer not havin' no job. Times're tough, 'specially 'round these parts since Union Carbide packed up, and then they closed the mine on account of the blammed Japs sellin' coal cheaper than we kin dig it. I makes enough green sewing boots so don't'cha worry none."

"Thanks, Grandpap," Travis gushed, his eyes still gazing down at the rotten floor. "But—" Travis' pea-brain thoughts stopped stock-still when Grandpap had come 'round the sewin' table. Grandpap, see, didn't *walk*, he *wheeled.* That's right, he wheeled hisself 'round that big cherrywood table, inna *wheelchair.* And that's when Travis spied that his fine old grandpap had no legs much past his knees.

"Grandpap!" he wailed. "What happened ta yer legs!"

"Aw, don't'cha worry 'bout that, son," Grandpap sluffed it off. "I'se old, an' couldn't get around much noways. Got some blammed fancified disease called *dyerbeetees,* so the doc down the state health clinic lopped off my legs. Swami fucker had the balls ta send me a bill too, kin ya believe it? But it ain't no big deal." Then Grandpap's skinny arm

15

extended behind him, to the rows of wood shelves full of his fine hand-sewn boots. "I kin still do my's work, an' figure I should be grateful."

Travis was impressed by his grandpap's resolve. But then the old man went on: "So how'd ya do in the poky?"

"Well, not too good, Grandpap. I hadda beat up on some fellas pretty bad, fer tryin' ta cornhole me, and there was this one fella tried ta make me suck his bone, so I stucks his prison shank in his eyeball and this stuff came out that looked just like the cranberry marmalade they sell down at Hull's."

Grandpap's creekbed face lit up. "D'ja kill him?"

"No, Grandpap, but I heard I stuck that shank in so far it got ta his brain and made him retart."

Grandpap clapped his liver-spotted hands. "Good fer you, boy! Yer daddy'd be proud, God rest his soul!"

"Anyways," Travis went on. He didn't like ta think about the slam, and he shouldn't have ta now, should he? There was still some ticks and tucks about it anyways, like something 'bout havin' ta report to a roll officer or some shit, but Travis didn't know nothin' 'bout that, and he didn't wanna worry 'bout it neither. It was just fine and dandy ta be outa that county cage full of shack bucks an' crackers and kiddie-diddlers. "I'll tries ta get me a job fast as I kin, an' in the meantime, Grandpap, I kin do stuff 'round the house to help ya out."

Grandpap smiled proud. "Travis, you're a fine young man, gracious, respectful, just like yer daddy raised, and I kin shore use a little help 'round here, seein' that I ain't got no legs no more. Like you kin bring in the firewood an' such, and haul the water up fer the squirrel stew and possum pie. Ya kin see—" Grandpap pointed to the floor just below the edge of his cherrywood work table. Travis noticed a strange darkness there, stained inta the wood, an' he remembered that from when he was little too. "Ya kin see," Grandpap rambled on, "that the floor's goin' all ta rot, so ya's kin help fix it, otherwise yer old Grandpappy'll be wheelin' across the blammed floor one day and—Kuh-RACK—that floor'll break right under my wheels an' drop yer poor grandpap right smack dab inta the fruit cellar."

"Oh, no, Grandpap," Travis exclaimed, "I wouldn't never want that ta happen! I'll'se be happy ta help ya fix the floor."

Grandpap wheeled closer, then, his smile turning dark. "An' there's somethin' else ya kin do fer me, son. Ya kin help give yer ole grandpap a thrill now an' agin."

"Shore, Grandpap, but . . . how?"

Grandpap snickered. "A'corse, I cain't do it myself no more, not with no legs, an', Chrast, take an old feller like me a coon's age ta even git his bone hard. But I'se still get a kick outa, well, you know . . . *watchin'*."

Watchin', Travis thought. He didn't quite get it.

"Headers is what I mean, son."

Headers, Travis thought. And that was somethin'—

"Grandpap," he said rather meekly, "that's somethin' I been thinkin' about since, well, since the day 'fore I got locked up." Yeah, it was true. *Headers.* "I 'member when I was little I'd hear you an' daddy sitting out on the porch talkin' 'bout it lotta times, an' right 'fore I wrecked Cage George's '74 'Cuda and broked Kari Ann Wells' back, I asked ya 'bout it. 'Member?"

"Shore I 'member, boy," Grandpap fired back keen-eyed. "An I 'member I didn't tell ya squat on account ya were too young."

"Yeah, Grandpap, but I gots ta tell ya now, it's somethin' I been thinkin' 'bout fer the whole time I was in stir. I gots ta know. What's a header?"

Grandpap's face, then, took on a look of something that some citified queer-lovin', pussy-wine-cooler-drinkin', banlon-shirt-wearin'-type might describe as ethereal. He wheeled a few inches closer in his rickety chair. "Ya know what, son, I reckon ya *are* old enough ta hear now . . . so's I'll tell ya."

Travis exploded in delight.

And Grandpap nodded. "Yeah, boy, I'll'se tell ya all about headers 'cos it's time you learnt. First thing ya need is ta snatch yerself a splittail, son, and the second thing ya need is this . . ."

And then Grandpap's shriveled hand reached out onto the table and picked up a power drill.

* * *

"A hundred bucks doesn't cut it anymore," Cummings said in his best bad-guy impersonation.

Spaz, long hair hanging in strings like greased yarn, shot him the funkiest of expressions. He grinned through bad teeth. "Shee-it, Stew, let me tell ya—"

Cummings' hand shot out, caught Spaz in a visegrip just under the throat. "First off, it ain't Stew. It's Agent Cummings. Understand?"

A little more squeeze, and Spaz nodded, puff-faced.

"Second, I ain't covering your hooch runs to the Kentucky line for a pissant hundred bucks a month. From now on, it's two-fifty."

Cummings released the grip; Spaz about fell.

"Hall ain't gonna like it."

"Then tell Hall he can shag my balls and lick my ass after I take a corn-shit. If two-fifty ain't square, then tell that low-life, moonshine-running scumbag he can find himself another federal cop to cover his runs. A c-note a month ain't worth the risk."

Cummings had been covering Hall "Shine" Sladder's unlicensed liquor runs for a year. They'd brew the stuff in a still up near Filbert—figured it was safer running a still in a "wet" state—then truck it over the line to Kentucky. Less heat. And *a lot* less heat when they had a Bureau of Alcohol, Tobacco and Firearms agent marking their routes for them and calling in diversions. But Cummings was baiting Spaz; he knew Sladder couldn't pay any more for his protection. It was in a roundabout way, instead, that Cummings was giving Spaz a push, because he knew Spaz was into more than backwoods corn liquor.

"You and Sladder are both skell, and you both know it," Cummings went on. "If you guys go down, you two pig-dick-lickers will spin on me faster than it takes you to pop a

18

butt-pimple. I need more green for my risk."

Spaz' hungover eyes fluttered as he to looked Cummings in the face.

"And if you chuckleheads even *think* about spinning on me, I hope you both have brains enough to realize I'll kill your redneck asses before you can turn evidence. So what's the deal?"

"Hall, he—" Spaz faltered in his smudged overalls. "He ain't got the dough, man—er, I mean Agent Cummings."

"You're not hearing me." And then Cummings drew his Smith & Wesson Model 13 chock-full of .357 Q-loads. Cocked it. "I need more money, and I can't trust you guys for shit."

"Wait, wait, man! Listen to me. Here's a deal for you. Keep covering Hall's hooch runs, keep taking the c-note, and I'll set you up with something else that'll pull you *a thousand a month.*"

Yeah. Got him. "In exchange for what?"

Now Spaz dared to grin. "Coverin' somethin' else, man. I run dust and pot too, and . . . coke."

"For who?"

"Fella named Dutch." Spaz was getting ballsy now. "You ain't need ta know his real name."

"So this Dutch motherfucker'll pay me a grand a month to feed him safe routes?"

"Well, yeah, I think so. It'll take me some talkin' though. I mean, Christ, you're a federal cop."

"No, Spaz, I'm a federal cop *on the take.* Tell this redneck piece of trash Dutch motherfucker that I can *guarantee* he'll never get pinched. I'm a fed, my office gets every state narc and DEA fax in the area. He'll sail clean as a cat's ass if he works with me. But I gotta have that k-note every month, in cash, unsequenced serial numbers. And tell him this too, Spaz. I won't just mark routes for him. I'll *carry his product* to his points in the trunk of my federal unmarked fucking police car. Tell him *that.*"

Spaz' moonshine-scarlet eyes grew wide in glee.

Cummings replaced his piece.

19

"Sh-sure, Stew—er, I mean, Agent Cummings."

"Cut out that Agent Cummings crap, will ya. Call me Stew." Cummings lit a smoke, offered one to Spaz. "We still friends or what?"

"Sh-sure, Stew."

"Just want you to know where I'm coming from. And this dope-peddler of yours, this Dutch—just think how happy he'll be when you tell him you gotta federal tin who wants to transport product for him."

"I-I never thought about it that way."

"Shit, Spaz, he'll be so happy with you, he'll probably pay your next semester's tuition at Harvard."

Spaz' face hooked up in confusion. "Whuh—what's 'harvard,' Stew?"

"Never mind. You guys need me to make your lives easier, and I need the bread. So go talk to your man. I'll meet you here same time tomorrow."

Spaz cheered up quick, smiled again with those teeth that would make a dental hygienist throw up in the rinse sink. "Tomorrow, man, you got it. Any luck I'll have your first month's dough in my pocket."

Cummings spewed smoke, nodded abruptly. "Talk to Dutch."

Spaz roared off out of the dell in his souped '71 Mustang, a 351 Cleveland. *Got him hooked,* Cummings knew. He'd played it just right, worked Spaz like a puppet and let him come to his own conclusions.

It was a beautiful day. He got back into his unmarked and pulled onto the county highway. *Yeah,* he told himself. *I'm a federal cop on the take.* He wasn't too happy about it, but how else could he afford Kath's medicine? In the past, it had just been hooch—no big deal—but now he was moving up to the real McCoy—coke, PCP, shit these scumbags sold to 9-year-olds, shit that turned people's lives inside out. But Cummings had a plan for that too.

Cummings was a Special Agent for the Bureau of Alcohol, Tobacco, and Firearms, Russell County Field Office, in Lewisburg, Virginia. He'd worked the gig 10 years now, busting bootleggers and moonshiners, busting stills, setting up stings. At first, he'd even believed in his work—until Kath had gotten sick.

I gotta come through for her, he thought desperately. *I can't let her down.*

Nobody else gave a shit, so why should he? And he swore to himself, once Kath was better, he'd go off the pad . . .

"Hey, Stew."

"J.L." Cummings dropped his gunbelt in the field office, hot weight off his waist. J.L. Peerce was the Special Agent in Charge of the FO, and he knew the ropes; Peerce grew up out here, was a rube himself until he got out and got himself an education. Slicked-back black hair, chopburns, and an Elvis sneer. Cummings didn't have much of a problem with him.

"We'se be goin' to Warshington next month, fer a training session at Buzzards Point," he declared. "Party hard in D.C. strip joints ever night, all on the lamb."

"Sounds good to me."

"So how was your watch?"

Cummings eased down in an opposing metal folding chair, lit up another Lucky. "Squat. Nothin'. Checked all those still sites we busted last winter, and the sites are dry. Checked all the back trails, and—nothing. But I'm finding a little activity in the some of the old McKully sites. Should be ready to drop hammer on them soon."

"Good," Peerce said from his own chair across a U.S. Government gray-metal desk. "How's the girlfriend, by the way?"

The question felt like a sudden fishhook sunk into Cummings' cheek. "The same. Goddamn medicine is killing me. Four-fifty a month, and it's going up."

"Don't knows how ya do it, Stew. Yer a good man."

Not as good as you might think, Cummings thought.

* * *

Ten years now, and all they were paying him was a piddly 32.5 a year. Different raise prerequisites and time-in-

21

service stats, save for a pissant COLA every now and then. Cummings reasoned it was their fault that he had to do what he did. If they paid him what he was worth—that would be different.

Wouldn't it?

The sun was sinking. State Route 154 ribboned through treelines and dead pastures, taking him home. Sometimes he had to pull over and masturbate—another thing he didn't feel too good about—because, despite his primal male needs, he knew it wouldn't be right to be going home and jumping Kath's bones, sick as she was. But whenever he did it, every single time, in fact, he thought about Kath . . .

She was always tired, always run down. He knew she tried hard to stay up for him every night, but lately she didn't even have the energy to do that. Sometimes she cried about it.

Don't think about it, he cut off the thought. *Be a man. Do the right thing. Take care of your woman, because you know goddamn well if it was you who was sick, she'd be bending over backwards to take care of you.*

That was about all it took.

He was about to take the turnoff when he saw the flashing red and blue lights up in Cotter's Field . . .

* * *

Travis lay back in bed, sighin' yet wide-eyed. Moonlight hung in the winder, and throwed light like purdy ribbons on the wood floor, and there were a ruckus of crickets and peepers.

Headers, he thought.

Yessir, he'd had hisself a mighty fine header tonight.

Grandpap had showed him how ta do it. A'corse, he'd hadda snatch hisself a splittail first, but that were easy. "Make shore it's from a fambly who done us wrong," Grandpap had instructed from his wheelchair.

Well, in the past, back when his maw and daddy was still livin', it weren't just the Caudills who'd gave 'em a bad time, jackin' their sheep an' all. One time, he remembert, a coupla Reid's dirty rube kids'd plucked all the apples offa one of Daddy's Golden Delicious trees, all 'cos a few branches had growed over the fence and were hangin' over the Reid's line. Daddy'd about had a fit. But Travis remembert that well, and when he were drivin' the pickup 'round, lookin' fer a splittail ta snatch, thar she was. He recalled her fairly well, Iree Reid was her name, and though she'd been a might younger last time Travis had eyed her, there weren't no foolin' him now, not with that shiny blonde hair or them big milkers stickin' out the front of her peach-colored halter. She were lopin' barefoot down the Old Governor's Bridge Road, and a'corse, bein' the gentleman he was, Travis pulled over an' offered her a ride home.

"Why's, you're Travis Clyde Tuckton, ain't ya!" she drawled her verbal celebration once she slid her purdy cut-offed jeaned backside inta the truck. "Why's I remember ya from way back when." Her purdy freckly face blushed a bit. "Don't mind tellin' ya now, I kinda had a fixin' for ya."

"Well I gots ta be honest, Iree," Travis admitted, "'Fore I got my butt throwed inta the county poky, I hadda mighty fixin' on you too!"

"Ya *did!*"

Travis slammed his big knuckly fist right smack-dab inta her forehead, and her little lights went right out. Then, pickup still rumblin', he tied her up but good, gagged her, and stuffed her curvy skinny body down inta the footwell. Next thing he knowed, he was carryin' her like a sack of farm feed inta Grandpap's work room, and took ta settin' her down on the big cherrywood table Grandpap made his boots on.

"One of them dirt-eatin' blondie Reids!" Grandpap exalted. "Good job, Travis! Now tie her down on the table and git them silly, whory clothes off her."

Travis saw and didn't even have ta be tolt, 'cos there was eye-hooks screwed inta each corner'a the table. Little Iree was still out fer the count, so Travis cut her ropes and tied her right back down to the table, on her back, her head hangin' over the table edge.

"What I do next, Grandpap?"

Grandpap tittered, stroked his whiskers, and wheeled right up ta the table. In one crabbed hand, though, he gripped the power drill, which were fitted with a 3-inch hole-saw.

"Travis, it's sorta like anything, anything takes practice, ya know. Like Thomas down the roadside bar? That ol' coot kin play the washboard just as pretty as you please, and Conga Powers, boy, he kin git ta pickin' the banja like nobody's business. Know why, son?"

The calculative powerhouse that was Travis' mind ticked right away. "Practice?" he guessed.

"S'right, boy. Practice. And as far as cuttin' open a splittail's coconut goes, I gots a lotta practice, I kin tell ya. Me an' yer daddy, see—and God rest his soul—we'se got ta be the best head-humpers from here ta New Orleens."

And with that fine testimony Grandpap squeezed the drill's trigger, paused, then applied it to the top of Iree Reid's purdy blond head.

Made quite a racket, it did, an' Travis' nose twitched at the smell'a burnin' hair'n bone, but it weren't another few more seconds 'fore Grandpap set down the drill.

"Yessir, a good 'un," he declared, and wheeled right up, inspectin' his job. "See that, Travis? What I done, see, is I cut me a perfect hole in the top'a her noggin. See?"

Travis leaned over, squinting. "Yeah, Grandpap. I see." And he also seed the perfect circle'a bone still wedged in the hole-saw. "So what now?"

"Just ya watch."

Travis, curious as he were, just clammed up and watched Grandpap, very adroitly now, push Iree's blond hair back, to show the fresh-cut hole more clear. Blood was drippin' a little onta the floor.

Then Grandpap picked up a knife.

"What'cha—what'cha gonna do with that, Grandpap?"

"Watch, boy. Gotta make a slit, fer yer pecker."

Later it would occur to Travis that this made sense. The knife was just yer typical steak knife, 'bout eight inchers

long an' one inch wide, and Grandpap, with the same surprise
expertise, stuck that baby right inta that hole in Iree's skull,
slittin' hisself a nice li'l slot. But, boy, once that knife were
retracted, out gushed the blood mixed with somethin' that
looked watery–CSF or cerebral spinal fluid, but a big dumb
animal like Travis wouldn't know nothin' 'bout that—and it
was then that Travis seed just how the floor at the base of the
work table got ta be so rotted. All that blood over the years,
pumpin' outa gals' heads, and the stuff just lay there, turned
the wood soft, an' went ta rot.

"Get'cher bone up, boy," Grandpap said, wheeling back
to watch and unfastening his trousers hisself. "Get 'er up and
stick it in. Have yerself yer first head-humpin'."

Travis didn't know quite what he thought about this at
first. Fuckin' a gal's *brain?* He dropped trow and jacked
hisself a tad, thinkin' 'bout some of the honeys he seed in the
girlie mags in the joint. An' once his dog was up an' barkin'
he stepped up to Iree's motionless head at the edge of the
table and paused.

"Come on, boy. What's wrong witch'ya? Ya got yerself a
header here, boy. Better'n any pussy ya ever stuck yer bone
in."

The implication was clear, a'corse: Travis were meant
to put his hard dick inta Iree Reid's head an' hump it.
Relucterant at first, he did so, but it weren't long 'fore he got
the feelin's.

"Aw, shee-it, Grandpap," his throat gusted. "This is
mighty fine, mighty fine, indeedy."

Travis held her dead head, humpin' it, his dog-stiff dick
plumbin' in an' outa Iree Reid's still-warm brain. At first he
thought it might be like jackin', in that he'd have ta think
'bout the girlie mags, and the gals he poled 'fore he went ta
the joint, or some of the butts he slammed whiles he was in
stir. No, Travis weren't queer, but when ya pulled 11 years
in the county slam, ya made considerations. Ever so often,
Travis'd get ta thinkin' and suddenly he'd be hornier'n a
field dog. So he'd find hisself one of the bitches (Bitches,
fer those'a ya that don't know, were what skinny boys was

25

called in the slam, and they was mostly always ready, willin', an' able ta spread their cheeks fer a pack of smokes or a li'l protection. And anyways, Travis helped hisself many a time, not that he were queer, mind ya, as has already been preeverissly stated. He'd just think about Kari Ann Wells' slick hot box whiles he's was doin' it, er some other gal he dicked way back when, an' he'd come just dandy.) But there weren't no need fer this now. *I'se havin' me a header! I'se humpin' a gal's brain,* he thought. *An' it feels GOOD . . .*

"Hump that head, boy. *Hump* it!" Grandpap goaded on from his wheelchair. "Give her brains a good squirt of yer jizz!"

And this Travis did 'bout a second later, huffin' an' puffin' an' humpin' away till the feelin's built up so bad, there were no turnin' back. He grunted then moaned long an' hard an' shot a gusher of his peckersnot deep inta the middle of Iree Reid's purdy head.

An' ya's know what?

It felt better'n any pussy he ever did hump, and any buttholes too. Fer shore. Travis, blushing and outa breath, stepped back an' let his limp bone slide outa the warm hole.

"Shee-it, Grandpap. You was right. Head-humpin's a kick!"

"Told ya so, boy," Grandpap obliged. He was jackin' hisself whiles he' was watchin, and had already creamed his belt buckle with a li'l spurt of his old man's juice.

"Ain't nothin' like a good header, Travis. No one been doin' it out these parts fer awhiles, but it's high time we'se get back ta the old ways. We'se gonna have ourselfs a head-humpin' most any chance we git, yessir! An' lemme tell ya somethin', son. Yer daddy'd be damned proud knowin' you just spewed a load of yer peckersnot in that blammed Reid girl's head!"

* * *

Cummings' mind felt aswarm with thoughts. First off, Kath, of course—run down all the time, lethargic, sick. But she still had a smile for him every night, didn't she? Then some harder things, like Spaz, and this dope peddler Dutch. He knew it wasn't exactly conduct becoming of a federal agent, but what else could he do? He needed the money. It wasn't like he was robbing banks, for Christ's sake, or taking down old ladies on Crotchett Lane for their social security. *I'm going to knock over a drug dealer, for crying out loud . . .* These guys sold crack to kindergarten kids. They put 13-year-olds out onto the street to turn tricks. They didn't give a shit about the kids, so why should Cummings give a shit about them? He'd be doing the world a service.

And as long as nobody found out . . .

I'm in the clear.

He'd just turned off State Route 154 when he saw the lights. Flashing *red and blue* lights. Croll's field, up past the dell. Cummings veered his federal unmarked up the incline, then stopped. A state police cruiser sat there, lights thrumming. Russell County was unchartered—no municipal departments and no county police either—couldn't afford it. The state responded to any major case.

Crickets tremoloed through the dell when Cummings got out. It was hot, humid. A full moon lazed over the treetops.

"Cummings, ATF," he announced. Though in his field uniform, he also flashed his leather-clad badge and ID as he approached the lean, whitewalled state trooper bending over a—

A dead body, Cummings noticed at once.

"Need any assist?"

The trooper rose and walked over, shaking his head. His face looked blanched as he lit a cigarette. "Thanks, but no. This one's over."

"What've you got?"

"Sig 64," the trooper recited. "White female, looks about 20. Dead for a few hours, looks like to me. I was heading back to my HQ for shiftchange, and there she was lying right there in my lights."

"What's the C.O.D.?"

"Blunt trauma to the head, it looks like."

"And it looks like she wasn't killed on site," Cummings remarked, shining his Streamlight on the corpus delectus. A pretty girl, young. Cutoff jeans and a halter lay aside. Pretty blond hair too. But he could see the hole in her head, and he could also see a suspicious lack of blood-saturation on the ground.

"Yeah, 10-to-1 some redneck did her somewhere else, then dumped her here. County coroner's on the way. I gotta wait till he gets here to secure the crime scene."

"Right. Good luck. Guess I'll be on my way."

"Thanks for stopping by to check it out. Shit, man, out here in the boonies—we appreciate it."

Tell me about it, Cummings thought. "Later." Then he tromped back to his unmarked and headed home.

* * *

"Shee-it," Cummings heard next morning when he entered the FO. The Russell County ATF Field Office was actually a 72-foot trailer located behind the bingo hall in Larchmont, and the hearty "Shee-it" had been uttered by Peerce. How a man the likes of Peerce had ever been promoted to Special Agent in Charge was beyond Cummings. *I'se from around these here parts, Cummings,* Peerce had bragged more than once. *I knows these folk up here, hows they think, hows they act, and I'se right good at sniffin' 'em out.* Jesus. The job of this illustrious three-man squad, of course, was to deter the manufacture of unlicensed alcoholic beverages—namely corn liquor—and to further deter its unauthorized distribution and sale. In a county where unemployment topped 40 percent, moonshine was big business. It was also, for whatever reason, illegal.

"What are you shee-ittin' about?" Cummings queried upon entrance. He set down his DOR log, his gunbelt heavy on his hip.

"Fuckin' state cops just wired us this 64." Peerce testily waved the fax, one side of his mouth bolus-like from the eternal wad of chewing tobacco. "Some cracker girl from

Luntville. 'FYI,' it says. 'Please file and note.'"

A 64 was a death report relative to suspected homicide. Frowning, Cummings took the fax and read it.

FM: VSP/VIOLENT CRIMES UNIT
TO: SAC/BAFT FO RUSSELL COUNTY/ IMMEDIATE
RECEIVING OFFICE: FYI, PLEASE NOTE AND FILE VIA FEDERAL LAW ENFORCEMENT COOPERATION ORDER. SHOULD RELEVANT INFORMATION BE BROUGHT TO YOUR ATTENTION, IMMEDIATELY NOTIFY VSP HQ
SUBJECT: REID, IREE, A. W/F DOB: 2 AUG 79 HAIR: BLD EYES: BR WT: 116 - VICTIM (DECEASED)

The date of file was late last evening. "Oh, yeah," Cummings offered. "State trooper found her in a field just off the Route; I talked to the guy. Said he saw her just lying there, was waiting for the M.E." Peerce made no reply, crow's feet around his eyes. Then Cummings read on.

PROFILING AND CONSULTATION: VICTIM FOUND DEAD VIA UNUSUAL CRANIAL INSULT, A 3-INCH OCULUS, APPARENTLY INFLICTED BY A POWER TOOL. MANMADE LATERAL RENT APPROX. 6 INCHES DEEP INTO CENTRAL SULCUS AND OCCIPITAL POLE OF THE BRAIN, PROBABLY INFLICTED WITH A KITCHEN-TYPE KNIFE WITH A DOWNWARD SERRATED EDGE.
NOTE: FURTHER AUTOPSY DIAGNOSIS REVEALS A PECULIAR PRESENCE OF HUMAN SEMINAL FLUID IN PROXIMITY TO THE INSULT.

Cummings' vision cruxed down on the stark fax paper. He'd seen plenty of strange state police wires in his time, but—*What in God's name is this?* he pondered.

"Cain't believe it. A fuckin' header."

Cummings glanced up. "What?"

Peerce was leaning over to retrieve his spit-cup. His previous comment had been more of a mutter to himself than something he'd said directly to Cummings. "I thought you were supposed to be gatherin' intelligence on McKully's stills?"

"Yeah," Cummings answered. "I got most of them tagged and marked; be ready to bust them any day. But what was that you just said? Something about a *header?* What's a header?"

Peerce sat down behind his dented, federal-gray desk, chawing fiercely as the sudden glint came to his eyes. "So how come you ain't out there now? It's tax dollars payin' your salary, ain't it? Don't be worryin' about no damn death report from the state cops. It's their 64 so let 'em handle it. Shee-it, McKully's probably just shipped out another truckload of 'shine while's you been standin' here jackin' your jaw."

"Come on, J.L. What the hell is a header?"

Peerce shot a staged gape at his watch. "You *still* here?"

Talk about avoiding the issue. True, Peerce was Cummings' superior, but he'd never given him the kiss-off like this. *A header?* Cummings thought, walking out of the FO to his unmarked.

The morning was blooming; the grand sun rose high over the mountain ridge. Pocked within that ridge, he knew, like termites in wood, were countless dozens of family stills run by the dirt-poor for generations. It was Cummings' job to sniff them out, or as was the case since Kath's illness, to let certain operations slide for a little grease, and to mark the liquor runs. *That's* what he should be worrying about. And he had something else to worry about too: tonight he was meeting with "Dutch." He was about to go to work for a dope dealer. *Get your mind back on the important things,* he told himself, and pulled the unmarked out onto the county road. Dust followed him like an amorphous contrail, something gaining on him.

But Cummings, stolid behind the wheel, couldn't shake it. For the rest of the day the question nagged.

What the hell is a header?

* * *

Yeah, Grandpap was dag shore right. Weren't nothin' like it. A header was far better a nut than anything he'd ever had. Nosiree. Weren't nothin' like it.

"Told ya, boy," Grandpap asserted from his wheelchair.

Gawd, was all Travis could think. Last night after he'd dumped Iree Reid's body in Croll's field, Travis had come home and gone ta bed an' he'd had ta jack hisself—twice, as a matter 'a fact—thinkin' 'bout how good it felt ta get his nuts off in that cracker girl's head.

"'S'how we do things 'round here, Travis," the old man informed, finishing the last needlestitch on the pair of boots he was workin' on. "'S'how we takes care 'a business. When someone does ya wrong 'nuff times, the only thing you kin do ta git proper revenge is havin' a header. Folks been fuedin' in these hills fer hunnerts 'a years. The Cullers an' the Canes, an' the Saltenstalls an' the Bessers, an' the Snoots an' the Meyers. And like your Daddy and that blammed Caudill over yonder, and folks been havin' thereselfs headers the whole time. An' it's only fittin' an' proper. Like it says in the Bible, son. An eye fer a eye."

Travis weren't too sure what eyes had ta do with humpin' people's heads but he just figured it was 'cos Grandpap was smarter'n him. And he didn't feel too bad 'bout Iree Reid, 'cos the Reids had shore done his Daddy wrong in the past, an' it must be okay 'cos, like Grandpap just got done sayin', it said so in the Bible it was okay ta head-hump folks.

"Now best you git on down the creek an' bring up some water, and git some more wood chopped," Grandpap ordered. "We'se gonna roast us up some of my good coon sausage t'night. And I got Nedder Kinney comin' up in a spell, the dog-dirty creeker, to pay me fer these boots I jus' made fer him. Ain't never liked the guy much, but his money's green so I'll'se take it." Grandpap lowered his voice. "And, 'sides, it's probably best you not be seen, son, on account of you're just out of the slam and busted yer parole."

"Okay, Grandpap."

Travis moseyed on out the back, down to the creek. Yes sir, it was shore good ta be out the slam. Fresh air, birds chirpin', the creek babblin'. Shore beat the cellblock, it did. *Good ta be alive weather,* his daddy used to say. And viddles? Grandpap could fix up some viddles like nobody's business. Possum Pie, Muskrat Burger, hot spicy stews, and, a'corse, that great chunky coon sausage. Chrast, that slop they served 'em at the cellblock looked like somethin' somebody'd upchucked into a pot and cooked it. It were a moment of self-awareness, it were, reverlations from God Hisself, tellin' Travis that he had hisself a dandy life, and Travis was rightly grateful fer it. Indeed he was!

Whistlin' to hisself, he brought up two buckets of water hangin' off the ends of a pole 'cross his back, but then he ducked a right quick 'fore he got back up the house, for he spied Nedder Kinney's ol' '74 Chevy pickup parked front of the porch. Grandpap was right; wouldn't be too good for Travis ta be seed, so he figured he'd just wait till Ned left. He remembert the Kinney's vaguely, lived in a couple shanties out past Kohl's Point, they did. Nedder had hisself a fat wife named Chessy, who had no teeth and got the tip of her nose bit off by a feisty squirrel once, and about half a dozen dirty little kids which Travis reckoned weren't so little no more on account of he'd been in the clink 11 years. Remembert Nedder ta be not exactly the nicest fella you'd wanna meet, ornery and half-crocked all the time from the 'shine he brewed in his still, an' meaner'n a shithouse rat. 'Corse, Travis figured he hisself'd be mean an' drunk all the time too if he had a wife as fat'n ugly as Nedder's, an' a bunch of dirty, snot-eatin' cracker kids, halfa whom he'd heard was retarts. But—

What was that?

Travis heard hisself a sound right then—

It's hollerin'? his pea-brain inquired.

But shore enough it were 'cos it got a tad louder next, and Travis knowed it was Grandpap and Nedder Kinney in there hollerin' at each other.

I wonder what's they'se hollerin' 'bout . . .

Travis edged up the side of the house, careful not ta make no noise, and then he put his big inquirin' face ta the screen, and there was big Nedder Kinney, his big smudged shoulders stickin' out bare from his overalls that shorely hadn't been warshed in a coon's age, and his rotten-toothed smile shinin' through a dirty beard. "You got's ta be shitting me, ya old stick, if ya think I'm gonna pay twenny bucks for these here boots."

"Blammit, Kinney!" Grandpap snapped back from his wheelchair. "Twenny's what we agreet!"

"Yeah, well I guess I plum changed my mind, ya crusty ol' cracker." Nedder wagged the brand-new boots in Grandpap's face. "These here're pieces'a shit, problee bust open on me inna week."

"Them's the finest boots in the blammed county, daggit! Won't find finer, long-lastin' boots nowheres, not even in one of the big city stores!"

Nedder Kinney laughed, flecks of stuff fallin' from his black beard. "Dumbest-ass thing I ever heard'n my life anyways, a fuckin' shoemaker with no feet." He slapped down a crumpled sawbuck. "I'se pay ten, ya footless old fuck, which is more'n a white trash old coot like you deserves anyways. Don't like it? What'cha gonna *do* about it?"

And with that remark, Nedder Kinney busted out a good guffaw, clopped out the house, and droved off in his pickup.

Travis felt a right bad, he did, lookin' in that winder and seein' poor old Grandpap sittin' in that blammed chair with just hairy stumps where his feet used ta be. Travis could 'magine his grandfather's frusteration, old, weak, can't walk or stand up. Folks could just rip him off any ol' time they pleased, because that stinkin' rot-tooth cracker galoot Nedder Kinney were shore right about one thing: there weren't nothin' in the world ol' Grandpap could do about it.

Naw, I reckon there ain't, Travis thought. *But there's shore's shit somethin' I can do about it . . .*

* * *

"So *you're* the big bad fed Spaz has been raving about?"

"That's right," Cummings said. "And you must be Dutch, the big bad dope runner."

Dutch had long blond hair and a hatchet face. Lean. Hard. A skull tattoo on his forearm. Cummings sat down in a dilapidated chair as Spaz brought out beers.

"And what's this deal of yours?"

"I'll make one run per week to your points," Cummings said, sipping cold Jax. "For a thousand bucks a month."

Silence dropped like a coffin lid. Cummings knew he had Dutch thinking. Spaz stood in the corner, a twitching shadow.

"Sounds good," Dutch eventually broke the quiet. "*Too* good, if you ask me. You're a fuckin' cop, man. Why should I trust you?"

"'Cos I'm the most trustworthy crooked cop in town. You think this is a setup? You think I'm wired? Search me. And ask Spaz. I've been covering his hooch points for six months."

"Yeah, Dutch," Spaz piped in, face ticking. He was probably on speed today. "Stew here's straight up."

"Straight up," Dutch mimicked. "How come a cop wants to work for a guy like me?"

Cummings' hands unfolded before him. It was time for his spiel. "Oldest reason in the world, Dutch. I need the money. I got a sick girlfriend who's getting sicker; each week she needs another medication that costs a fuckin' arm and a leg, and the bread the feds pay me wouldn't buy a good box lunch. I been bending over backwards for the ATF for 10 years, and I haven't even gotten one promotion, while everyone else in this shit-stinking world makes out like a bandit. Now its *my turn* to make out. Fuck it. I'm going on the pad. You don't want to work with me, fine. I'm sure I can find some other dope dealer who'd like to have a federal cop in his pocket."

The look on Dutch's face broadened; the point, obviously, drove home. "One run per week to my points, and a thousand a month in your till?"

"That's right."

Dutch's steely eyes leveled. "How much product per run?"

"As much as you can stuff into the trunk of my federal police car," Cummings answered.

Dutch eased back in his chair, lowering his beer in a lax grace. Then, for the first time, he smiled. "I think we can work with this," he said.

* * *

"Hump that head, boy!" Grandpap wailed. "I say *hump* it!"

And Travis, he humped it like a trooper, he did, that big cherrywood work table thunkin' with each hump. Travis' bone never felt so hard in his life, no sir, as it were right now slidin' in an' outa Chessy Kinney's head as she lay like a sidled-over Berkshire hog on the table. Travis had seed her pickin' raspberries just 'fore nightfall, big as a Berkshire hog herself inna puke-green sundress, all big tits an' belly strainin' against the flinty material, ratty brown hair hangin' in ropes 'round her fat face. Travis had offered her a ride home in his pickup, then jacked her out but good with his brass knucks once she gots in. It just hurt him so bad seein' the crushed look on Grandpap's face after that dirty, hoochin', dick-cheese-eatin' Nedder Kinney had pulled that stunt, only payin' a paltry sawbuck fer a pair of Grandpap's fine workboots. But it were like the Bible said, a eye fer a eye, 'er somethin' like that, so Travis felt it letgitermat ta snatch Nedder's fat, cracker wife and have a header.

He'd brought her back ta the cottage and slugged her down belly-up on the table, huffin' an' puffin' on account she weighted more'n a wheelbarrow chock fulla wet cee-ment, and Grandpap, when he seed what Travis had done, just up

35

shouted with sheer fuckin' joy, skinny arms raised high. "Ain't that just the finest grandson I been blessed with!" he exclaimed.

"Well, Grandpap, I figured it was fittin' after seein' the way Nedder Kinney ripped ya off fer yer boots," Travis reckoned. "Weren't right what he did, so we'se'll get him back proper." Travis, then, set ta makin' the hole ta slide his peter in, and a question occurred ta him. "Hey, Grandpap, lets me ask ya somethin'. Weren't it be easier, 'stead goin' ta the trouble'a workin' the hole-saw with the drill, ta just knock a hole inner head with a good ballpeen or pig sledge?"

"Naw, boy, and lets me tell ya why," Grandpap, in his erudite wisdom, replied. "Hammer don't make a clean hole, an' that's a mite important. 'Member Sisal Conner, fat sack cracker lived in the lean-to out by Watter's Pond? Fer *years* he dropped pigs fer William's Meat Company, 'fore they closed it a'corse, on account'a the 'conomy. Anyways, Sisal were an expert at crackin' skulls, did it eight hours a day, an' he could drop 'em pretty as you please. Then, once Williams laid his tired ass off, he got to cuttin' wheat on the government subsidy, an' I 'member one time one'a the Croll boys sugared the gas tank on his brant-new John Deer thresher, so Sisal just snatched one of the Croll kids a week later, see, an he invites me an' yer pappy over fer the header, an' insists on usin' a ballpeen on account he was so expert with it from his pig killin' days, an he smacks that boy a tad too hard, picks the pieces out best he could and puts his peter right in. Caught a bone sliver, son, right in his dick knob he did, an' next thing we know he's runnin' 'round screamin' with blood squirtin' out his stiffer like he's takin' a red pee. So that's why ya don't never use a hammer, boy. Ya always use the hole-saw 'cos there weren't never be no bone splinters ta catch a hitch in yer dick."

Wow. Folks were right. Old folk knowed what they was talkin' 'bout, an' if there were one thing Travis didn't need, it was a bone splinter slidin' right inta his dickmeat. No sir, he didn't need that none at *all!*

So's Travis, then, rememberin' the technique, screwed

the hole-saw inta the power drill and got ta openin' the top'a Chessy Kinney's head. Tears of glee shined in Grandpap's old, rheumy eyes whiles Travis were doin' the job. Made a hell of a racket, it did, but in less time than it take ta blow a snotwad out'cher nose, that little circle of bone popped right out, an' Travis didn't waste no time stickin' the knife in the hole ta make a good deep slit fer his pecker, and when he did just that, even though ol' Chessy were still unconscious from the brass knucks, her fat and kinda hairy legs kicked up once, and that was that. She were dead on the table, deader'n dogshit.

Blood poured out her head like tappin' the bilge drum onna hot hooch tank, but once all that cracker blood got out, Travis got in—with his woody, that is, and a might good it certainly felt humpin' that still-warm cracker brain'a hers. Travis kept his eyes closed whiles he was doin' it 'cos he didn't wanna be ganderin' Chessy's body, no sir. What a mess of a woman she was, rolls'a fat jigglin' under that stinky dress, her big dirty feet stickin' out over the opposite edge'a the table. She had big tufts of hair unner her arms which reminded Travis of the balls'a steel wool he'd hafta clean pots with on chow hall duty in the slam, and one'a her tits popped out just then, big as a baby's head it was, an' it just kinda lolled there like a bag'a chicken fat, and a coupla skanky black hairs stickin' outa a nipple that looked more like a bloody hock someone'd just spat. No sir. Travis didn't need ta be lookin' at that 'less he wanted ta lose his woody right there inner head.

"Hump it, Travis!" Grandpap rallied on, now pink-faced as he was jackin' hisself in the chair. "Get that nut *right up* in her head, boy! *Hump* that cracker!"

Well, hump that cracker Travis did, an' it didn't take long. Travis felt the feelin's buildin', and they was like no other feelin's he'd ever felt. Travis' eyeballs crossed, they did, and he grabbed Chessy Kinney's big dirt-seamed ears an' humped harder he did, an' it was almost like that knife-slit in her cracker brain were a hot suckin' mouth onna five-dollar roadhouse whore, and right then, Travis went up on his tiptoes, and he blowed hisself a long an' hearty nut inta the middle of Chessy Kinney's corpus callosum, not that Travis hisself knowed just what a corpus callosum were, nor did he know what a central sulcus 'er a occipital pole were either. Suffice ta say, he blowed hisself a long, hot dicksnot right inta the middle'a her cracker head, an' it felt a right good, it did. Ain't come that good in his life.

"Aw, shee-it, Grandpap. Lemme tell ya, that was one *dandy* nut!"

Travis stepped back, slick with sweat now, and he let his limp pecker slide right outa that newcut headhole.

"Yeah boy!" Grandpap agreet. "Headers're somethin', ain't they? Who needs poon when ya kin hump a head?"

"But—Grandpap." Travis stalled, feelin' a might guilty. All this time he was havin' so much pleasure fer hisself, and there was poor Grandpap, with his old bone still hard an' stickin' up outa his lap.

"Shee-it, Grandpap. You ain't had yerself yer own nut yet."

"Aw, no matter, boy. Ol' coot like me, takes a while it does. Just watchin's fine enough. Watchin' a strong young man like yerself humpin' a head, reminds me'a the good ol' days, and lemme tell ya son, I humped myself a fair share'a heads."

"I'll'se bet ya did, Grandpap," Travis concurred, zippin' up. "So why's don't ya hump yerself a head right now? Got a fresh one right here on the table, we do, if ya don't mind no sloppy seconds."

"Aw, shee-it, son. I 'preciate ya thinkin'a me, but my head-humpin' days're over. Cain't stand up outa this blammed chair. Ain't gots no feet on the end'a my legs."

Travis smiled a great big warm family-lovin' type smile. He knowed a way, he shore did!

"*I'll'se* be yer feet, Grandpap," he said, and his big brawny, muscular 28-year-old arms hoisted Grandpap right outa that blammed chair an' walked him over ta Chessy Kinney's dead white trash head. "Ain't no way my Grandpappy's gonna sit by an' watch me have a header but him not." Travis hoisted the ol' man outa that chair like he weighed no more'n'a duck-feather piller. "No don't'cha worry 'bout me turnin' queer in the joint, Grandpap, 'cos I ain't no queer, but I'se got ta grab yer pecker a sec, ta guide 'er in." And then Travis took a quick grasp'a Grandpap's stiff root, still holdin' the man up with but one arm 'cross his chest, an' he guided that ol' feisty bone right inta that waitin' wet hole in Chessy's redneck head.

"Aw, Travis," Grandpap wheezed in unearthly delight. "Cain't tell ya how good it feels ta have my dog inna gal's brain after all these here years."

"Go fer it, Gramps," Travis urged. "Hump that head! *Hump* it! Get'cher'a load'a yer peterjuice right up that hole!"

Wizened as he were, Grandpap humped, held kindly aloft by his good, strong grandson.

"Take yer time, Grandpap. Cream her head up good, goes ahead! Hump it!"

Grandpap's flat ol' butt pumped away, an', old 'er not, it didn't take more'n'a' couple of minutes 'fore he was gaspin' an' shudderin' an' shakin' like a leaf in orgasmeric bliss. "Ooo-yeah, ooo-doggie, yessir!" his ol' throat crackled. "Aw, shee-it, Travis, I'se spunkin' up her brain fierce! Got enough cockhock in my's ol' balls ta fill a blammed shit-bucket!" Spittle dribbled inta his white billygoat beard, and Grandpap's roadmap eyes rolled back in his head. "Aw, it's just the best feelin' in the world, it is! Chrast, boy, I just pumped me *whopper* of a load!"

"Good fer you, Grandpap!" Travis commended. "You shore showed that blammed Nedder Kinney fer rippin' you off. Done had yerself a nut in his *wife's head!*"

Travis set the old man back in the wheelchair once he was done comin'. But at once Grandpap just set there, an' he looked up at Travis and started cryin'.

"Aw, shee-it, Grandpap. What's wrong?"

"Boy," Grandpap wept freely, and then his Adam's apple bobbed as her swallered. "That, I say, that is goodliest thing anyone ever done fer me in my life . . ."

Travis wiped a big booger in Chessy Kinney's ratty

white trash hair, and he smiled with pride that he'd done somethin' ta make his grandfather so happy. "The ways I sees it, Grandpappy, is whiles I was in the stone motel, there's was a lotta hillfolk out here who done my fambly wrong, an' like you said, when someone does ya wrong, it's only fittin' an' proper that ya do 'em wrong back. Say's so in the Bible, don't it?"

"That's right, son, it shore does. An eye fer a eye, it says."

Travis weren't lookin' forward ta luggin' this big 250 pounds of cracker trash out ta some field, but he'd worry 'bout that later. "An' since so many folks in these parts done dag dirty things over the years ta my fambly, I say we'se gonna have ourself quite a few headers fer quite a spell. How's that sound, Grandpap?"

Grandpap's crinkled face fell to his open hands, and he cried on in sheer happiness. "Thank ya, God! Thank ya fer blessin' me with such a fine young grandson!"

Travis nearly cried hisself seein' his grandpap so delighted. He hunched down an' slid Chessy Kinney 'cross his back. "I'll'se be back in awhiles," he bid. "Gots ta dump this stinky fat cracker in the woods somewhere, I do," he articulated. "Hope the possums don't mind eatin' stinky redneck fat."

* * *

It wasn't the thousand a month; cops on the take never lasted long. But Cummings knew he'd played it right. He'd work his way in slow, get to know the turf, the points, and the scumbags in charge of them. No way this Dutch dude was going to start him off driving large orders of primo product. It might take a few months, but Cummings would prove his worth, and he'd keep his ears open while he was doing it. Never touch any of the bags of product, so he didn't have to worry about prints, and whenever he drove a run, he replaced his federal-issue Smith & Wesson Model 13 with his unregistered Webley revolver. If things got hot one night, and Cummings had to pop caps, he wouldn't have to worry about any ballistics striations that could be tied to his service piece. So that's how he played the gig. Eventually, he'd get wind of a big drop, and—

Well, he'd think about the rest later.

He'd set the meal tray up in Kath's lap, got her settled into the lounge chair in front of the TV. She hadn't touched any of her dinner.

"You should eat, sweetheart," he said. "You need your strength."

Her tired eyes fluttered. "Oh, honey, I'm so sorry you went to all this trouble to fix dinner. But I'm just not hungry at all. I can't eat."

"That's all right," Cummings said. "Maybe we should go to bed now. You look tired."

All Kath could do was nod.

He'd clean the dishes later. He picked her up, wan in her nightgown, and carried her to bed. But just as he got the covers over her, he noticed that she was crying.

"Honey?" His hand lovingly touched her cool cheek. "What's wrong?"

She hitched and sobbed and sniffled, blinking up at him. "Stew, I'm so sorry. I should've told you but I didn't. I know how hard you work as it is. But—"

"But, what, Kath?"

Her pretty face looked flattened when she finally told him. "Dr. Seymour's putting me on another antibiotic. And it costs—it costs—oh, Stew, I'm so sorry!"

The poor girl. She was so sick, yet she didn't even have the courage to reveal the cost of the medicine that might cure her.

"It's going to cost another three hundred a month, along with what you're already paying for the others."

Ordinarily, Cummings would've wilted. But that's not what his girlfriend needed to see, was it? A man collapsing against the weight of a grim reality. The thousand a month he'd be raking from Dutch, plus his hooch protection for Spaz' people, would more than cover the added pharmaceutical expense. So all Cummings did was smile.

41

"Don't worry, sweetheart," he was happy to be able to say. Then he lied, but it was a white lie, wasn't it? "I finally got that promotion today."

He knew it took all the strength she could muster to squeal with delight and wrap her thin arms around him and kiss him. Feeling her lips on his, after so long, made his heart surge, and it revitalized his love.

"Stew, I'm so proud of you," she whispered.

Jesus, if she only knew, he thought. But that didn't matter. He was going to shake down a drug dealer. So what? He was doing the only thing he could do to help the woman he loved.

"Baby," she hushed, pulling at him. "I know haven't been much of a girlfriend these past months, and—"

"Don't say that! You've been sick. It's not your fault."

"—and I know I'll get better soon, and I'll make it up to you. But right now—" Her voice turned sultry, her whisper drenched with passion. "Right now—" Her hands felt hot on his neck. "Right now . . . I want you to make love to me."

Cummings nearly ejaculated in his pants at the words. He loved her *so much,* and it had been *so long.* But he also knew that her words were preemptory. She was too sick. She'd never be up to it.

"I want to too, honey, but you need your rest," he said, and it wasn't easy, not after masturbating in the bathroom or in the car for six months. But how considerate would that be? Climbing on top of his sick girlfriend? "You're going to get better real soon, I know you will, especially with this new medication. Then we're going to go on a second honeymoon that'll knock your socks off!"

"You're such a wonderful man," she murmured, but already she was falling asleep.

Cummings went back downstairs, washed the dishes, cleaned up a little. He cracked open another beer and changed channels to the Yankees' game—when the phone rang.

It's fuckin' 10:30 at night! he objected.

"Cummings," he said into the phone.

"Yeah, Stew, look, I been out here two hours, man, and I'm dog hungry."

It was Chad Amburgy, the night man. Decent kid, if a bit redneck. Done Cummings several favors.

"Out where?" Cummings asked.

"Kohl's Point. I was on reglar patrol, gonna check out McKully's old haunts, see if he was putting back anymore stills, when I saw it, so I radio'd the state."

Cummings blinked, shook his head. "Saw what, Chad?"

A crackling static pause; Amburgy had obviously radio'd the state dispatcher and rerouted the trans through the phone, via a landline hookup. "We got another murder out here, Stew. And gawd knows how long it'll take these state police nimrods ta get the M.E. out here. How's about givin' me a break and bringin' me out some samwiches or somethin'. Anything, man. I'se starvin' out here."

"Kohl's Point you say?"

"Yeah."

"Hang tight, Chad I'll be there in twenty."

"Thanks, man."

Kohl's Point, Cummings thought, strapping on his gunbelt. He whipped up some quick sandwiches in the kitchen, brewed a thermos of coffee, and grabbed an extra pack of smokes.

We got another murder out here, the words echoed in his head. Christ. And then more words fluttered, like slow, black birds.

Peerce's words.

Cain't believe it. A fuckin' header.

Cummings couldn't have known, of course. Nevertheless, he was sweating pretty bad when he got into the unmarked and headed, lights on, to Kohl's Point.

* * *

"Thanks fer comin' out, Stew," Chad Amburgy obliged, his stomach stressing his ATF field shirt. He plowed into the bag of sandwiches.

"So what've you got here?" Cummings asked. He slipped his Streamlight out of his belt.

"Some fat lady, hillfolk probably, as ya can see. Just saw her layin' here, Stew, when I was comin' up the Route. Blood all caked in her hair."

"But no blood under her head," Cummings noticed, adjusting his beam. *Just like last night.*

"Must've been killed somewhere else and then dumped here."

"Yeah." *Just like last night.*

Amburgy munched a BLT and chugged coffee right out of the thermos. "I didn't have too close a look, didn't want to risk messin' up the crime scene." Amburgy pronounced *crime* as *cram.* "Peerce told me to radio the state and wait for 'em. Pretty pissant job of body-dumpin' though. Just dumped her flat out in the middle of the field."

Yeah. Just like . . .

Cummings carefully hunkered down, aimed his flash beam right on top of the decedent's head, which was a mess of caked blood. With a pencil end, he pushed aside some of the clotted tresses, to reveal the insult.

"Yeah, someone cracked her good in the head," Amburgy postulated.

"Not cracked. Drilled."

"Huh?"

Cummings let it pass. A perfect circle had been cut out of the top of her skull, exposing the keenly slit brain. More macabre words came back to haunt Cummings . . . *a peculiar presence of human seminal fluid.*

And, again, Peerce. *A fuckin' header . . .*

"You check the perimeter for tire tracks?"

"Naw, not much. Dirt trail right there at the treeline. Must've been where he drove in. But the trail's dry."

Cummings cast his light. No, there'd be no impressions left there. He'd leave it for the state to look at. At least the semen in the head could be typed, for all the good that would do, and they could run a g/p scan too, and their toolmarks lab could try to possibly make the brand of the hole-saw, but Cummings doubted that the state police criminal evidence section would bother. This was just a cracker murder to them, a fly-by-night.

"What the hell is that?" Cummings asked when he stood up and roved his Streamlight again. A yard off from the victim's feet something glistened.

"Looks like . . ." Amburgy leaned, his cheeks stuffed as he chewed his sandwich. His nose twitched. "Looks like a pile'a dogshit or maybe a horseflop. Looks like it's been—"

Cummings nodded. There, satcheled amid weeds, clearly lay a deposit of some kind of animal excrement, and said deposit just as clearly had been—

"Damn right, Chad," Cummings observed. His Streamlight glared down. "And it's been stepped in."

* * *

Peerce glanced up, glanced at his watch, then glanced up again from behind his desk at the FO. As discreetly as possible, which wasn't very discreet at all, he slipped this month's issue of *Babes With Big Boobs* under his desk blotter.

"Ain't like you ta be three hours late ta work, Stew."

"Didn't you look on the op log?" Cummings sniped back. "I was 10-6 to Millersville."

"State Sub HQ? What'cha doin' there all morning?"

Some Special Agent In Charge, Cummings complained. *Doesn't even read his own operating report.* "It's right there in the log, J.L. I was 10-6 to Millersville, on an evidence check. That 64 Amburgy stumbled on last night? Identical m.o. to the Reid girl the night before. Only this time the perp left a footprint."

"Oh yeah?" Peerce replied without much interest.

"Stepped in a pile of dogshit, left a perfect impression of the bottom of his right boot."

"Some hayseed steps in dogshit and you take it to state police CES?"

"I photographed it. Showed it to their tech and got a pattern layout. Was hoping they'd be able to match the pattern to a manufacturer's solescheme in their computer."

"What the hell fer?" Peerce asked, more absurdly now.

Cummings rolled his eyes. "Finding out the manufacturer

of the boots would give us a list of local outlets. Might be able to narrow down the stores in the area, check invoices, get a clerk who remembers, that sort of thing. If we have a list of the stores that sell the boots, we have a list of areas the perp might live in."

"Wastin' yer time, Stew."

"Oh? They'd already run an electrophoresis test on the semen in both heads," Cummings challenged. "The perp's bloodtype is A pos, subtype Mn. But there's A pos *and* B pos in the second head, the one from last night. What's that tell you?"

"Nothin' of importance." Peerce was barely listening now. He even retrieved his copy of *Babes With Big Boobs.* "You tell me, city boy."

"It tells us that *two* guys ejaculated in the second head." Cummings caught himself there, realizing exactly what he'd just said. *Ejaculated in the second head. I've got two perps out there somewhere who've cut holes in the skulls of two women, and then they . . .*

He didn't finish the thought.

"It ain't squat, Stew," Peerce insisted. "What good's knowing the perp's bloodtype?"

"I can run a records sweep now, check out any A pos Mn ex-cons or psych-ward releases in the area. It's something."

"It's *squat*, Stew. Yer pissin' in the wind. And what about the footprint?"

"The state evidence tech ran a digitalization of the print pattern in their comparison computer. They've got every tread scheme of every shoe or boot ever made in the country. She knew it was a boot due to the sole-depth. But there was no match."

"See? Squat."

"Which tells me that the boot was handmade, which'll be even easier to check out. Get a line on any local shoemakers, and I got a line on the killer."

Peerce looked up again, trying now to play Boss Man. "Ain't you got more important things ta do? Like stake out McKully's land fer more stills? That's yer job, ya know, not playin' Dick Fuckin' Tracy on a coupl'a no-account cracker murders."

"I'm a fuckin' cop," Cummings profaned in reply. "*My job* is to investigate criminal activity."

"Yer job, Stew, is ta bust stills—"

"And that leads me to my next question." Cummings sat down, took a breath. Peerce, low IQ notwithstanding, was his superior. He couldn't get *too* shitty.

"You're not leveling with me, J.L." he said.

"How's that?" Peerce asked without looking up from the tit mag.

Cummings caught a glimpse of the mag. A blonde was spraying milk into a redhead's wide-open mouth. He blinked away the image, cleared his throat. "What's a 'header'?"

Peerce slapped the mag closed again. "Aw, shit, man! Just leave it, will ya!"

"No. I want to know. That's what you said under your breath after the state sent the fax on the Reid girl. A 'header,' you called it. What the hell's going on?"

Peerce spat tobacco juice into his obligatory cup, then pinched the bridge of his nose as if attempting to tamp a migraine. "Cain't you just leave shit be?"

"No. What's a header?"

Peerce opened his hands on the desk, leaned back, sighed. "It's just somethin' that goes on, is all, somethin' folks don't talk much about. It's nothin'."

Cummings looked aghast. "J.L., we've got at least two men in our juris who are *cutting women's heads open* with a hole-saw and *fucking their brains.* That's *nothing?*"

Peerce faltered further, grimacing like stomach gas. "If you was from around these parts, you'd know what I meant. It's feuds, boy."

"Feuds?"

"Yeah. Feuds." Peerce spat out his lump and loaded up another chaw of Red Man. "You wants ta know, city boy, then I'll'se tell ya. Cultures're different, see? Everwhere ya go. The Serbs hate the Bosnerians, the Jews hate the Ay-rabs, the Japs hate us."

Cummings' frown blistered on his face. "What's that got—"

"And 'round here," Peerce drawled on, "everbody hates ever-one else, fer all kinds'a reasons, from way on back. Don't matter why, just is."

"All right," Cummings gave him. "Feuds. Fine. The Hatfields and the McCoys."

"Right, Stew, only in these parts it's the Crolls and the Watters, the Lees and the Ketchums, the Kleggs and the McCrones, like that. It's universal, Stew, just different in different places. Someone shits on ya, ya shit back twice as hard, see? Gets ta the point when ya cain't one-up each other. Understand?"

"No," Cummings responded. "Answer the question. What's a header?"

Another spit, another sigh, then Peerce came clean. "A header's the worst thing these rubes out here could think of. It's like the law of the hills. Someone does ya wrong bad enough, then yer justified ta do the worse thing imaginable fer yer revenge. That's what a header is. Folks don't talk about it much, it's just somethin' that's understood. Yer gettin' all whipped up 'bout somethin' that's been going on fer generations."

Cummings closed his eyes, took a deep breath himself now. "J.L., you're telling me that that's what this is all about? Hill people feuding? Cutting holes in women's heads and—"

"That's right, boy, so don't'cha gripe 'cos you was the one who asked. It's one-uppin', like I said. Someone slashes yer tires, you burn down his barn, then he rapes yer sister, and you kill his son. When there ain't nothin' left ta out-do the other . . . ya have a header, ya throw a head-humpin'. Ya snatch the other guy's wife 'er daughter, get the boys together, an' then ya hump 'er head. Like that. I growed up in these parts, so I oughta know. 'Round here, there ain't nothin' worse ya can do ta someone than pull a header on one of his kin."

Cummings stared. His mouth attempted to form words but failed.

"That, Stew," Peerce finally verified, "is what a header is. 'Round here, folks take care of their own, so that's why there ain't no need fer you ta be blowin' tax dollars at state CES tryin' ta run down bloodtypes an' fuckin' bootprints. Just a bit unusual that the perp'd leave the bodies where anyone could see 'em. Yoo-sherally they'll leave 'em on the property of the fucker that done 'em wrong in the first place."

But Cummings was still staring. Was this madness or what? *Headers,* he thought baldly. *Head-humping. My . . . God . . .*

* * *

And head-humping it would be.

Over the next seven weeks, no less than a dozen more 64s were reported, same m.o., same autopsy findings. Some of the victims were identified, some were not. It didn't matter. But what did matter was that on all occasions, the brains of the corpus delecti were found to contain liberal amounts of A Positive and B Positive semen, and on two more such occasions, bootprints were found with an identical tread-pattern.

Ever the dutiful law-enforcement officer, Cummings pursued the crimes.

He also pursued the ill-gotten gains of driving point for Dutch the Drug Dealer.

This divide in Cummings' sense of human purpose didn't obscure him. The continuous head-humping murders amounted to something whose evil he could scarcely comprehend, and he felt it was his professional obligation to stay on the case. And as far as Dutch went, well . . . that was different. Once a week, Spaz beeped him on his Motorola pager, and Cummings was there. He had a sick girlfriend to think of, after all, and the drugs—namely PCP, marijuana, and cocaine, mostly cocaine—would be sold and distributed anyway. ATF Special Agent Stewart Cummings could not possibly hope to stem the flow of illegal drugs.

But he *could* solve the head-humping murders, couldn't

he? It was his *duty.*

He'd put in for countless evidence scans and records checks with the state police. He knew it would take time, but Stewart Cummings was a patient man, and, they said, patience was a virtue. So, he'd wait. And in the meantime, he'd drive his unmarked federal police car, with Spaz as his guide, to various "points," his trunk loaded with controlled, dangerous substances. He'd unload his shit, in other words, and take his grease, to keep afloat in a rocky world and provide his girlfriend the necessary monies for her innumerable medications. And on the side, he would vigorously investigate what he now thought of as The Russell County Head-Humping Murders.

Slow but sure, leads were made, but a bit more quickly, Kath's maladies worsened. She couldn't even attempt to get out of bed before noon, whereupon she'd drive to the doctor's, then drive to the local pharmacist's, procure her meds, and just get sicker and sicker. Acute Temporal Pneumonia, the doctor's diagnosis continued to affirm, with symptoms of related seasonal affect disorder and acute hypoglycemia. Kath's love for Cummings, though, never waned. He could see it in her eyes, he could sense it in her aura, and Cummings knew that one day soon, she would be better and their lives together would resume as they'd dreamed. They dreamed the same dreams most couples did. These, after all, were Cummings' promises to her. A crew of children, a white picket fence and a two-car garage, a collie in the yard. He would give her all of these things, once she was recovered.

And until then—

I'm doing okay, he realized. *I'm covered.*

Though Kath's medical and pharmaceutical bills went up, so did Cummings' pad. Soon he was pulling $1,500 a month for driving Dutch's points, not to mention the continued peanuts for covering the transport routes for Spaz's hooch supplier. Cummings was paying for all of Kath's meds, plus the everyday bills, plus putting a little away into savings. And there was one thing he avowed to himself.

When Kath gets better, I stop.

Cummings actually believed this, and maybe it was even true. But he remembered his priorities, as well as his golden rule: Cops On The Take Always Get Caught. Which was why, as he'd previously planned, he would seize any "special" opportunity, and maybe have the chance to put enough in CDs to cover Kath's medical expenses just in interest. Then he'd be clean and wouldn't have to worry. And there was another thing: whenever he and Spaz delivered product to a point, they carried back a bag full of cash. Ten thousand, fifteen, one time *thirty-five.* Cummings wasn't stupid. Eventually, he knew, he'd sufficiently gain enough of Dutch's trust to drop point on a *really big* score. Then—

I'm made in the fuckin' shade . . .

But the headers carried on. A dozen became two dozen, then three. They were finding the bodies on the shoulder of Route 154, for God's sake, and in culverts and ravines, in wide-open fields, all over the place. Same m.o. each time. Same perps.

Cummings' judicial curiosity smoldered. This was his sideline, all right. He was going to solve the head-humping murders if it took everything he had.

And then, one day, he got a break . . .

* * *

"Hump that head, boy. *Hump* it!"

Travis pumped away, this time on Betty Sue Morgan, whose pappy had once swiped sheep from Travis' own dad. She was sweet an' young, with flowin' clean red hair and a *nice* set of milkers on her. Purdy cooze too, but Travis, by now, weren't interested much in cooze. Best pussy in the land weren't nearly as good as a nice hot brain.

"Aw, shee-it, Grandpap!" Travis postulated. "My bone's so hard it feels like it's gonna *bust!*"

"Then let it bust, son! Bust a nut right'n'side 'er head!"

And this Travis did, almost as if on command, squirtin' a good-sized pecker-loogie right inta the soft pulp'a Betty Sue

Morgan's deliciously warm gray matter. It was a fine nut, it was, an' a generous one. 'Fact, Travis' jizz felt like a coupla big worms beltin' out his peckerhole.

"Your turn, Grandpap," he said, and, as were the case ever-time now, he picked his grandpappy up under the arms and held him up. Grandpap humped away, he did, railin' an' rejoicin' as his bone were shuckin' hilt-deep in an' out'a Betty's purdy head. And when Grandpap gave her his squirt, he cried, as he yoo-sherally did now, heaped with gratitude fer what his one an' only grandson were doin' fer him. Helpin' ta retrieve his younger days, he were. And what greater gift could a grandson give his grandpappy, huh?

An' once that final load'a dickjuice were fired straight up inta Betty Sue's head, Travis, sated as a tom cat after etin' a mouse, hauled her purdy dead ass out the truck, and droved off ta dump her. A'corse, purdy as she were, Travis' bone was hard agin 'fore he ever made it out ta the Route, so's he hadda pull over, an' thought he'd give her poon a last shot'a the salt fer good measure. Humped her dead pussy hard, he did, and fer a long time, but it were nothin', so's then he took a good hock 'tween her buttcheeks and humped her cornhole—but still . . . nothin'. Just weren't nearly as good, 'n fact, as humpin' her head, no sir. So' that's what Travis did next, lay her flat out on the hood'a the truck, an' stuck his root right back inner head. Humped her so hard, 'n fact, there's was milk spurtin' out her big creamy tits, on account of she just dropped a li'l white trash crumb-snatcher a few months back, he'd heard, and once Travis were done pourin' his last nut inta her head, he'd worked up quite a thirst, he did, so's he shook the last drops outa his cock, then he leant over and took a good long suck off those great rib melons'a hers, and had hisself a *fine* drink'a milk. Tasted kinda sweet and still warm, it did, and it were probably a full quart he sucked out of 'em by the time he were done. Her tits looked smaller, comes ta think of it, once he were through, 'bout plain-ass sucked 'em dry. Then he dumped her dead ass off by a big pin oak tree offa Tick Neck Road.

Yeah, head-humpin', that were it. Nothin' better ta relieve the stresses of day-ta-day life, no sir. Get a fella off just dandy it did. And it were only fittin', on account'a these gals, and a coupla times fellas, were all kin ta folk who done his Daddy wrong. So Travis, driving back down the Route under a high moon, an' peepers makin' a ruckus from the trees, had hisself a moment of self actualization.

A eye fer an eye was what the Bible said, and that could be interpreted as meanin' it was alls right ta head-hump a neighbor who done ya wrong. So's by head-humpin', Travis rightly figured, by squirtin' his daily big load inna gal's head and havin' hisself a dandy nut, he were also follerin' the word of the Lord, doin' a service ta Chris-cher-anity. Ain't that right? Was a mighty great God who'd smile on those fer humpin' heads, yes sir!

But as he droved the pickup back to the cottage, Travis got ta thinkin'. This last month 'er two, he'd pretty much got back at all those who screwed his dear dead Daddy over. Gots back at the Reids an' the Kinneys an' the Watters an' the Shoals an' the Smits an' Gawd knowed who else. Weren't many left ta have a header with, 'n fact. But that last nut in Betty Sue's head still left him tinglin', an' just thinkin' 'bout it got him another stiffer right quick, so's he unzipped whiles he were drivin', he did, an' jacked hisself off a last nut an' wiped the watery come off on his shirt, an' then he got back ta thinkin'.

I gots ta know, he truly did declare to hisself, the high moon in his eyes, and his mind a'swayin'. *I gots ta!*

Yes sir. I got's ta have me a talk with Grandpappy . . .

* * *

Kath was remorseful, crying. "Oh, honey, I just can't stand myself!"

"Sweetheart," Cummings implored, next to her in bed.

"I'm just so *run down* all the time . . ."

"It's that acute pneumonia, honey. Dr. Seymour wrote it all down on the diagnosis. It'll pass. Eventually all those

53

medications will take care of it. Don't worry darling. You'll get better."

"That's not what I mean," Kath sniffled. "I'm just such a crummy girlfriend to you—"

"Don't say that, Kath!"

"—I can't get up till noon, I can barely do the shopping or clean the house, I can't even make love to my husband!"

"Kath! Don't worry about it. You're sick."

"Yeah, but for how much longer? You work so hard for me, and I can't do anything for you! One of these days—"

"What?"

She sniffled again, sobbing into the pillow. "One of these days you're going to leave me, and I wouldn't blame you!"

Cummings stroked her hair, rubbed her back. "Honey, honey, I'd *never* leave you. Never. I promise. You'll get better soon, and everything will be all right. In the meantime—"

Cummings' darker half spoke up. *In the meantime, you greased pig, you'll carry coke for a dealer . . .*

"In the meantime," he said, "I've got it covered. That raise—"

What raise, you lying asshole? The only raise you've ever gotten is from a coke peddler. Give yourself a slap on the back, buddy. You're running product for the same people who sell crack to teeny-boppers . . .

"—that raise I got at work will take care of us fine. So don't worry."

She sniffled on, hitching under the covers. "You're so good to me. One day, I promise, I'll make it up to you, I swear." Then she feebly dragged the sheet up over her rump, and pulled up her nightgown. "You can if you want. I want you to, darling."

Cummings felt like a cad. Here was the love of his life, sick and despondent and crying, yet offering herself for his pleasure. He couldn't. Enticing as her backside looked, he *couldn't . . .*

"Sweetheart, go to sleep now. There'll be plenty of time for that later, when you're better."

"You're such a wonderful man," she murmured, and then

drifted off.

Cummings covered her up, then padded to the kitchen. Oh, yes, it had been a long time, his erection was proof. He stood in the dark, in front of the kitchen sink, and masturbated, shucking his penis like an ear of corn. He could imagine how he'd appear to any onlooker: A grown man, a *cop*, beating his meat over the sink. Nevertheless, he orgasmed rather quickly, then sighed. The lines of his semen lay like white slug trails in the bottom of the stainless-steel sink. He turned on the faucet, washed it all down the drain, like the gravy off of last night's salisbury steak TV dinner . . .

For the whole time, though, he'd thought only of Kath, in her past days of beauty and voraciousness, and never of anyone else. Now that he was a "drug runner," many "opportunities" came his way. Junkies and shack hags and groupies, all hanging out at the drop-points, and all offered for his pleasure. Some of them weren't bad looking. They came with the trade.

But each time, Cummings declined, thinking of the real things in life, and his real promises. Driving point was one thing. Fucking junkie whores was another. He'd wait instead, sipping beer and smoking Luckys, while Spaz knocked the bottom out of them, his speedfreak face twitching . . .

He could've cried himself just then, that part of him which condemned what he was doing.

What else can I do! he exclaimed.

No answer was forthcoming.

He went back to bed and lay in the dark, Kath asleep at his side. He gazed up into the abyssal darkness as though it were the face of every mystery of humankind. The nightsounds— spring peepers, crickets, hoot owls—seemed to merge with the icy moonlight streaming in through the window, to form a *different* sound, a more subjective one, a sound that only his wide-open soul could hear. The sound of the deepest chasms, or of the highest places of the earth . . .

And still more sounds haunted him when he drifted off into fitful sleep. The sound of nightmares . . .

Jesus . . .

The sound of a power drill fitted with a three-inch hole-saw. The sound of muted screams, and of bone smoking under 2500-rpm steel teeth. The sound—

—yes!

The sound of faceless hayseeds, of anonymous backwoods rednecks, chuckling as—

—as—

—as—

Jesus Christ, get me out of this dream!

—as heads . . .

Were humped . . .

The sound was *evil.* The sound was *darkness,* the uttermost darkness of the human mind. What could be conceived of more dark than this?

Humping . . . heads?

And the sound descended, a funnel to hell, fricatives and sibilants and murmurings as black as anthracite, as black as the gaps in the molars of the devil, and as black as his thoughts—

Cummings roused from his dredge-like sleep, as though touched by a cattle prod.

The phone was ringing.

* * *

Cummings met Beck the next morning, answering her late-night summons. She was an odd-looking woman, with ashy hair and a voice like someone with sinusitis, about forty. Jan Beck was the deputy field chief for the state police criminal evidence section. "Wild, huh?" she asked.

"I could think of more appropriate terms," Cummings replied.

For the last month, he'd been processing technical requests, and now, finally, they were being answered. "It's strange, all right," she said in her lab. She leaned against a Vision Series V blood analyzer and lit a cigarette, openly ignoring the DO NOT SMOKE IN THIS LAB sign. Shelves of glassware flanked one side of the brightly lit room, while various machines—gas and liquid chromatographs, mass-photospectrometers, Kodak fingerprint processors—flanked the other. "But you have to admit, the hills are a strange place. It's like another world."

"Tell me about it," Cummings nearly laughed. "I've been busting stills out in the sticks for years. But last night on the phone—you said you had something."

Jan Beck nodded, exhaled a plume a smoke. "Couple of things, actually. First off, I've got an ID on your perp."

Cummings simply stared at her words, his face becoming deranged.

"But don't get a hard-on in your pants just yet." Beck stubbed her butt out in a petri dish. "It was funny. You've been processing tech requests for quite a while. Yesterday I get an inter-office memo from Records saying that ATF had asked for a rap sweep on any cons recently paroled from the slam or popped from the state mental hospital."

"I processed that request a month ago," Cummings pointed out.

"Hey, things take time, and that's not my point. Records gave me one name: Travis Clyde Tuckton. Did 11 years in Russell County Detent on a GTA and involuntary manslaughter."

Cummings didn't quite follow her yet, but he wrote down the name in his pad. TRAVIS CLYDE TUCKTON.

"Then," Beck continued, sitting up on the top of a Sirchie iodine fuming cabinet, "Hair & Fibers calls me up. They put a full UV and IR scan on any grievous 64 we get piped through the Body Shop. What they found was a dried semen smear on the girl's right breast."

"Yeah?" Cummings bid.

Jan Beck's face remained deadpan. "The smear had a fingerprint in it. Dry. Perfect."

Cummings' heart suddenly thumped beneath his ATF tunic. He didn't have to ask, he didn't even have to goad her further.

"So we UV'd the print and photographed it, ran it through the Cyrix digitalizer, and then sent it through Triple-I at the

Edward Lee

State Bureau of Investigation. Took all of 20 seconds to spit out a latent match."

Cummings' eyes went wide as slot-machine slugs.

"Travis Clyde Tuckton," Beck said. "Some coincidence, huh? And Tuckton is A Pos Mn with 4F non-bar-bodies, same as the semen we've typed in every head."

"It's him," Cummings croaked. "I've got to—

"Save it. Tuckton got popped from county detent several months ago, skipped his parole officer the first minute. So we sent a goon squad to his last place of residence, and, guess what? It was burned to the ground, from years ago. Nothing there."

Cummings' shoulders slumped. "So now it's needle-in-the-haystack time, huh?"

"Yeah. But at least you know your perp's name, and you know what he looks like."

Jan Beck handed Cummings a thin manila folder. Cummings blew off cigarette ashes, opened it, and gawped.

An in-pross photo. Hayseed just by looking at him: the kid had short black hair, slicked back, rubeburns, a big friendly farmboy-redneck grin and innocent brown eyes.

"If you hadn't pushed this," Beck pointed out, "we never would've bothered doing the forensic workups. We got a homicide guy on it now, but don't expect much action."

I hear that, Cummings thought. State wasn't going to put much manpower into a bunch of hillfolk murders, however bizarre. "Looks like its up to me."

"Good luck," Jan Beck offered. "Hey, and keep me posted, will ya? Can't wait to read the details when you catch this . . . head-humper."

"You got it. Thanks." Cummings made a quick exit from State HQ. He felt exhilarated. Look at what he'd done. He'd shagged the crime scenes, processed tech requests, and now he had his own investigation going on a real crime, not rednecks running panther piss but a sexually motivated, multiple homicide case. For the first time in a long time, Cummings felt like a cop.

But when he got back into his unmarked, his pager went

off. It was Spaz.

"Yeah?" Cummings asked when he dialed up from a QWIK-STOP payphone.

Spaz sounded tittery in tense excitement. "We gotta run to make tonight. Big order, man. Meet me at Dutch's. We gotta enough blow to sink a ship."

* * *

Jory Slade, according to Grandpap, had once whupped his Daddy's butt in a bar fight down the Crossroads, back when Travis were just a tike. Busted a few of Daddy's teeth, Jory Slade did, an' took his wallet too. An' worst'a all, Grandpap recited, when Slade were done with his ass-kickin', he laughed high an' might, and peed right in his Daddy's face. An' seein' that this injustice had gone unallayed fer so long, Travis felt it only proper now ta snatch one'a the Slade girls—a sassy li'l splittail named Sarah Dawn who turned tricks up the Bonfire Truckstop. Travis had parked way in back and eyed her fer a spell, and when she were hoppin' out a' a Peterbilt cab, he just up an' grabbed her, hauled her inta the truck. "Don't'cha make no noise," Travis promised, his big hand 'round her neck, "an' I won't hurt'cha." Well, you know what she did? Hocked a spitter right in Travis' face, and it weren't just noise she made, it was a *infernal racket*, it was; her little yap opened right up like a hay-drop, an' she let outa scream so high Travis thought his blammed windshield might crack, so's he put the squeeze on her throat an' that's was the end of her ruckus. Put up a hail of a fight, though, fer about another minute, flailin' an' kickin' fierce as a muskrat inna trap, and one'a her feet caught Travis in the crotch, an' he almost shouted out hisself, it hurt so bad. But he kept the squeeze on, an' 'ventually her face turnt kinda dark pink, like possum belly after ya skin it, an' her little lights winked right out.

"Good thinkin', boy," Grandpap approved, settin' down his awl an' leather-puncher from the next set'a boots he was makin'. He cleared off the work table fer the business at hand. "That be one'a the Slade girls, ain't it? Kin tell by the big space 'tween her eyes, on account her maw drunk a coupla jars'a shine ever day while's she were preggered. Popped out eight kids like that."

"Shore are right, Grandpap. She's a Slade all right," Travis respondered, not in the best'a moods since she done took that spit in his face an' that kick ta his 'nads. He tied her down ta the table but good with some good sisal rope. Yoo-sherally he didn't bother 'cos he kilt 'em quick, but he tied this feisty whore down on account he was so mad. "Kicked me in the balls, Grandpap, and they'se'a achin', an' she spit in my face ta boot!"

"Low-down dirty cracker bitch, she is. Looks like a whore, 'n fact, in them dirty shorts'n halter."

"That she is, Grandpap. Caught her turnin' tricks up the Bonfire. Did six 'er seven guys in their cabs just in the hour I'se was watchin'."

"Yeah, boy, a low-down cracker whore, I shoulda knowed. Jory Slade got eight kids in all and not one of 'em did he raise right. I ever tell ya 'bout the time Jory sucker-punched yer paw at the 'Roads? Beat yer Daddy's ass bad, he did, an' then peed in his face."

"Well, yeah, Grandpap, you done told me 'bout that just this mornin'. That's why I snatched his daughter." Sometimes, see, Grandpappy's memory didn't serve him best these days.

Travis tied her down extra tight, determined ta do a really special job on this one. One thing ya don't *never* wanna do is kick a fella like Travis in the nads, 'er hock in his face, 'cos that'll get his dander up like stick-pokin' a weasel ya got cornered in the henhouse.

Grandpap's face beamed in approval as he looked on. "Yeah, bet this whore's got enough nut up her cooze an' inner belly ta fill a pig trough."

"She's gonna have more'n that inner *head,* Grandpap," Travis celebrated, "time we'se through humpin' it!"

He poured Grandpap an' hisself each a shot'a corn, an' waited, an' whiles they was waitin' he yanked offer top 'cos he liked ta gander a gal's tits now an' agin. Hers was kinda small, though, with nipples that looked like they'd been chewed, an' ordernarily, he would'a yanked off her shorts too, ta have a look at her bush, but he didn't dare 'cos he shore didn't want all that trucker nut sloppin' outa her hole onta Grandpap's fine worktable. Weren't long, though, 'fore Sarah Dawn Slade come to, whereupon she set out ta screamin' an' cussin' like the devil hisself. "I knows who you are!" she wailed at Grandpap in his chair. "Yer Jake Martin, you is! Just a dirty, booger-eatin' ol' cracker with no feet! An' you, *you*—" Her big wide redneck eyes shot right ta Travis. "Yer Travis Tuckton. Heard they turnt you queer in prison, I heard! Heard you been suckin' cock an' gettin' butt-fucked with a big smile on yer face fer the last 10 years!"

Travis were not inna good frame'a mind ta begin with, and these low-down remarks only stirred up his piss-off all the more. He felt his face turn dark with anger, an' his eyes cross, an' he slapped his big hand right down on her haughty face, dug his fingers inta her cheeks till her yap opened wide as a wellhole, and then he coughed hisself up a dag *big* loogie an' dropped it right smackdab inner mouth. "There ya go," he said, then palmed up hard on her chin an' held it till she had no choice but ta swaller. "There's somethin' good fer ya ta eat. Oughta go right nice with all that trucker jizz in yer gut." But when he let go, she kinda bucked and then throwed right up.

"Aw, shee-it, girl!" Travis yelled. "Ya done upchucked all over my grandpap's fine cherrywood table!"

An' upchuck she did, high an' might, hoistin' it all up right out her mouth like a bilgepump, leavin' a big puddle'a bellyslime an' sperm, with Travis' big loogie floatin' right in the middle of it all.

"Don't'cha worry 'bout the mess, son," Grandpap excused. "We'se kin clean it up later. But fer now, let's get on with the work." Then he passed along the drill, an' the hole-saw bit were already screwed in.

Travis kept her quakin' head steady with his right hand, an' cut the hole out her head with his left . . .

61

Ain't much point in relatin' any further details, just ta say this were the best header yet. Travis an' his grandpap humped her head four times 'tween the two of 'em, and by the time they was done, their peckers had about whipped Sarah Dawn Slade's cracker brain ta porridge. Grandpap murmured in happiness from his chair, and even Travis hisself was exhausted from such a fierce head-humpin'. Yessir, he hadda lot'a angst ta work out, an' this cracker whore were just the ticket. But his mind kept'a tickin', it did, as it had been doin' quite a bit of late, goin' over all the injustices'a the world, an' then he thought back agin ta what Grandpap had told him, 'bout how Jory Slade had not only sucker-punched his Daddy and beat his butt, but about how Slade had also peed in his Daddy's face while's he was down.

Travis stood up.

"What'cha doin', boy?" Grandpap inquired, wipin' up all that puke an' trucker cum from the table. "Ya just had yerself two nuts inna row. Yer bone hard *agin?*"

"Naw, Grandpap," Travis answered. "I gots ta pee, an' I cain't think of a better place to do than this gal's head. After all, Grandpap, her daddy peed on my daddy, so's this is only proper."

"An eye fer a eye, boy!" Grandpap rallied.

Travis slipped his limp bone right back in that warm hole, then leaned back an' pulled a long, hard, hot corn-liquor pee. Yes sir, he whizzed away inta Sarah Dawn Slade's head fer a *good* long time, he did . . .

* * *

It's . . . the motherlode, Cummings thought.

"It's 10 keys, 80 percent pure," Dutch said matter-of-factly. He sat down in a beaten recliner, popped open a beer. Inside the shack, the humidity felt thick as broth. "I told you our point orders would be getting bigger."

Spaz was giggling aside. Cummings just stared. On the table lay a veritable *mountain* of bagged cocaine.

"You get *five grand* for the run," Dutch said. "Just do like you usually do. You and Spazzie load it up into your little police car and drop it off on our guy in Big Stone Gap, then come back here and you get *five grand.*"

Cummings struggled to clear his head. He had to play the game right. A swig of beer, then he turned poker-faced to Dutch. "This is a huge run and you know it. I'll take the cash up front or it's no deal."

"Somehow, Stew, I knew you'd say that." Dutch tossed a wad, which Cummings caught in the air. Fifty rubber-banded $100 bills.

"See, Stew, I'm a businessman. Since I hired you to drop for me, I haven't lost a single order. And when that happens, my distro goes up and so do my long-term points. We'll be getting an order this big every week. And you know what that means?"

"What?"

"You just got yourself a raise to twenty grand a month."

Cummings was sweating. All this time he'd been waiting for his ship to come in. Well here it was: the fuckin' Queen Mary. Twenty grand a month for making one drop a week. That was serious money. That was one sweet deal.

But the universal rule came back to haunt him.

Cops on the take never last long . . .

Cummings wasn't stupid. He could drive point for a few more months, rake in some dough, sure. And every day was another chance to get burned. This was the moment he'd been waiting for; he'd known that all along, just hadn't really admitted it. These 10 keys were an initial drop, and Cummings knew that Dutch took half in advance. And he also knew this: there was only one way for any cop on the take to get out clean and fat.

"Okay, Spaz," he said. "Let's get this blow in the car and get moving." When Spaz grabbed the first couple of bags, Cummings shucked his off-duty Webley .455, and—

BAM!

Spaz' head erupted like ripe fruit. Dutch rolled out of the chair, ducked, then sprang up with a cocked Glock 9mm. But Cummings was expecting this, and—

BAM!

—caught Dutch in the throat before he could get off a single shot.

Silence, then.

Hot fumes tickled Cummings' sinuses. The entire move was so automatic it nearly surprised him. He kicked the Glock out of Dutch's hand, squeezed off a point-blank headshot to be safe, then reholstered his piece. The Webley's irredeemably large projectile reverted Dutch's head to a plume of pink-red crap blown across the floor. *I just killed two guys,* the realization unfurled, *and I don't care.*

He checked the windows. Nothing. Then he looked back at the cocaine. Ten keys would have an astronomical street value, but there was no way he could handle that. He'd made the right move, he knew. This was his clean break. Besides, it wasn't the coke he was after.

Yeah, that fucker takes half on delivery. I know he does.

He searched the place. It didn't take much effort. *It's the Queen Mary, all right.* In the back room was a gym bag—full of banded hundred dollar bills.

He kept his cool, lit a Lucky, stood a moment to think. His future was set. Never again would he have to sweat Kath's pharmacy bills, and never again would they ever be in want. He'd have to be careful how he spent it, just a trickle at a time, and he knew he couldn't put it in the bank, for that would alert the IRS. *Be smart,* he told himself.

He couldn't leave the cocaine, either. He needed this to look like a dope hit, and hitters would never leave 10 keys of 80 percent blow on the table. So he threw the gym bag in the trunk, then loaded up the coke. He'd used his Webley to smoke Spaz and Dutch, a precaution that paid off—with the Webley there'd be no remaining ballistic evidence to tie Cummings to his service piece, his Smith 13. There'd be a few of his fingerprints in Dutch's crib, though, but the can of kerosene in the utility shed would take care of that. Way out here in the boondocks? It'd take an hour before anyone even noticed the smoke, and by the time they got a county firetruck out here, there'd be nothing left but a pile of cinders and two flame-broiled redneck pieces of shit.

So—

All bases were covered.

Cummings drenched the bodies and the front room with kerosene, lit the trailer line from the porch, then got into the unmarked. In the rearview, the shack burst into flames.

Cummings drove off and never looked back.

* * *

"All right, son, out with it," Grandpappy insisted that night. They was sitting out on the porch, sippin' corn and gazin' out upon the beautiful world Gawd had given 'em ta gaze upon. The sun was sinkin' low, throwin' dapplin' light through the trees, evenin' embracin' 'em. Birds raised Cain up in the high branches, and owls were beginnin' ta hoot. It were a beautiful comin' night, it were . . .

But Travis sat dejected.

"Come on, boy," Grandpap reasserted. "Somethin' buggin' ya, has been fer weeks. So's why don't'cha tell yer ol' grandpappy?"

"Aw, shucks, Grandpap." Travis' eyes remained glued ta the porch-slats. He'd sound like some prissy puss, he would, whinin' ta Grandpap 'bout his misgivin's, conjectures, an' mental wanderin's'a late. Earlier, he'd dumped Sarah Dawn's deader'n'a fencepost body offa one 'a the old county roads, left the low-down dirty whore there ta git et by possums, which were what she deserved fer what her pappy did ta his own. And Travis'd hoped that the extra-rowdy head-humpin' they'd pulled on her would set his mood back on track, get him outa this subjecterive slump he'd been lingerin' in. It didn't though. Two nuts an' a good, hard pee inner noggin', an' he were *still* feelin' in the dumps.

"I'se just," he began. Then: "Shee-it, Grandpap. I dunno. You'd think I were a big blubberin' pussy if I tolds ya what's botherin' me."

"Lemme tells ya somethin', son. 'S a time when *all* men feels like pussies when they's gets ta thinkin' 'bout sentimental-type shit. Ya know, stuff like where we fits inta God's plan, an' what's we mean in the large scheme'a things, what's we'se mean ta the unerverse an' all. And, a'corse, when we gets ta thinkin' 'bout our loved ones who's passed on. Bet that's it, ain't it, boy. Yer troubled 'bout yer maw an' daddy, ain't that right?"

It were amazin', the level of Grandpap's perceptiveratee. 'Cos that were it right on the head! "Just feel bad, all them years I'm in the clink. Never got ta help 'em, never got to share proper in the joys'a life. I'm sittin' in the poky fer stealin' a car an' my fine folks get kilt inna wreck."

"Don't'cha worry none, son. Yous turnt out just fine, yer a fine boy an' yer maw and daddy'd be proud'a ya."

"Aw, shee-it, Grandpap," Travis reiteratered. "It's just—I dunno. It's just that the whole thing don't feel right, ya know? Like there were more ta my folks' dyin' than meets the eye. Cain't properly 'xplain it."

"Well, Travis," and Grandpap looked a might sullen all at once, his feisty face goin' dark behind them whiskers. "I gots ta admit, son, yer quite right about that."

Travis looked up. "What'cha mean, Grandpap?"

"I nevers told ya on account I figured ya didn't need ta know. Yer life been tough enough, bein' in the slam an' all, and I figured ya didn't need me makin' it no tougher by tellin' ya the truth about how yer folks died."

"Tell me, Grandpap!" Travis stood up and about begged. The porch shuddered at his mere standin'. "I *got's* ta know! Won't feel like a whole man if I'se never know the truth!"

"Simmer down, boy," Grandpap consoled. "An' I'll'se tell ya."

Travis swigged the last of his corn, then sat back down. He were sweatin' an' all prickly. He *knowed* somethin' were wrong 'bout the story, an' he *hadda* know what went on fer real. "Please, Grandpap," he nearly whimpered. "So it ain't really true? Maw and Daddy didn't really get kilt in a car wreck?"

"Son . . .well . . . It's sorta true. Lets me start at the beginnin'. You knows at least 'bout how yer paw hadda feud runnin' with the Caudills, who owned mostly that shit land just north'a here, which yer daddy sold 'em fer a song years back. Namely a dag cracker bastard named Thibald Caudill. Had two boys, an' his wife died droppin' the second. The boys thereselfs both died too, when yous were in stir, 'cos when ol' man Caudill gots money, the first boy turnt queer an' died'a the AIDS, an' the second, he just up an' dropped'a hair-in addiction, 'er cocaine 'er some such, one'a them hippified drugs, an' as far as Caudill hisself goes, well, we tried not ta let you know a lot 'bout his feud with yer daddy, 'cos it weren't healthy fer a young boy bein' raised in a feudin' environment. But it's Thibald Caudill, boy, that's where the story begins. Short, fat little cracker, ory-eyed most nights drinkin' corn. Tried raisin' sheep fer the longest time but never made much outa it. Made more, I 'spect, stealing yer daddy's sheep."

Travis listened right hard, on the edge'a his seat. "Thibald Caudill. I 'member Daddy cussin' up a storm many a time 'bout him, but don't recall the man."

"That's 'cos he moved ta Pulaski, oh, five years 'er so 'fore ya got sent up ta the stone motel. Ol' Caudill, he's got hisself a fancy mansion now. He's a millionaire, on account'a that land he bought fer shit from yer daddy. Worthless junk land we all thought, an' then one day Caudill offers hunnert bucks an acre, so yer daddy took it. Next thing we knows, there's natural gas found on it, Caudill discovered it *before* he made the deal, ripped yer daddy off bad, but some of the land, see, the few acres Caudill *didn't* buy, had gas on it to, so we think we'se sittin' purdy 'cos we still had the deed fer those acres."

"Then—" Travis' big curious eyes widened. "Then how comes we ain't millionaires too, Grandpap?"

Grandpap's face got all fulla mean lines then. "'Cos Caudill, what he did was he sent one'a his boys to bust inta the house one night when yer maw and daddy were at the fambly reunion up in Filbert, an' he plumb stoled the deed."

"No!" Travis wailed.

"'Fraid so, son, an' he got some fancified city printer ta doctor his own deed, sayin' he owned all the land."

"No!"

Grandpap were visibly disturbed recitin' this story, so's he took a breather then an' poured hisself some more corn. "That's the long an' short of it, son. Both Caudill *and* yer daddy could'a been fair millionaires, but Caudill wanted it all, he did. Anyways, yer daddy and me, and yer Uncle Helton and a few others, we'se put all our scratch together ta hire ourselfs a big city lawyer from Roanoke, but 'fore we could, that's when yer maw an' yer paw got kilt. An' whiles you were in the slam, boy, ya know what Caudill did, just fer shits an' giggles? 'Member when I'se wrote ya at prison, tellin' ya how lightnin' struck yer house? Well, it weren't no lightnin', son. Caudill paid someone ta burn down yer old house too. Just fer the fun of it."

Travis had tears'n his eyes, hearin' this. What a awful world it were, that such things could happen, an' what a right bastard God was fer lettin' evil folk like the Caudills exist. It weren't fair, it simply weren't fair!

"He comes out here ever now an' then, Caudill, I mean, drivin' 'round in a big silver Rolls Royce. Ever coupla years er so. Just ta have a laugh at all us, I 'spect. Just ta show off that he got ever-thing an' we'se all been left with nothin'. But I'se realize all that still don't properly 'splain what really happened ta yer folks, so if yer's ready fer it, I'll'se tell ya."

"I'se—" Travis' throat hitched from his tears an' sobbin'. "I'se ready, Grandpap."

"One night yer maw an' paw was drivin' back from Roanoke, from the lawyer's, an' it was late, an' they was comin' offa the Route onta the Tick Neck Road, an' next thing they knowed, a pickup were tailin' 'em. It was Caudill an' his two boys, and they drove yer daddy right off the road, they did, inta a oak tree that were as wide as you are tall, son. Yer daddy got shot right out the windshield, he did, an' lost his head on the way. An' yer maw . . ."

"She died in the wreck too, huh, Grandpap?" Travis reckoned.

"No, son, she didn't." Grandpap steeled hisself. It were obviously gettin' to him, recitin' this awful story'a tradgerdee an' greed an' murder. "She were wearin' her seatbelt, son, whiles yer paw weren't. It weren't the wreck that kilt her, no sir."

Travis was nearly shudderin' in lamentation. "What, then, Grandpap? What happened, if it weren't the wreck?"

"It was those evil, devil-lovin' Caudills, it was, son. An' what those varmints did—" Grandpap paused fer another nip, his throat dryin' out. "They—they—"

"*What,* Grandpap?"

Grandpap's eye homed in on Travis', tears an' all. "It kills me ta tell ya this, son, but what they did was this: those devil, dag-bastards pulled yer maw outa the car an' they—they— well, Chrast, son. They tored her clothes off, butt-fucked her each right there on the hood'a the car, an' then they . . . Aw, God, it pain's me so ta say it! They had thereselfs a header, boy! Those cracker bastards done *head-humped* yer maw!"

Travis cried an' cried, he did, an' when there weren't no more tears left, he just up an' passed out right there on the porch, screamin' in his dreams 'bout what the blasted Caudills did ta his maw an' paw, but 'specially his maw. Head-humpin' her! The lot of 'em!

Those dag bastards head-humped my maw! Travis wailed in his sleep fulla the awfulest dreams . . .

* * *

Next day, Travis weren't much fer talkin', no he weren't. Grandpap neither, 'cos recitin' last night's story put a case'a blues on him somethin' fierce. "I'se sorry, son," was the only thing he said ta Travis. "I'd'a tole ya sooner, 'cept it didn't seem right ta say such horrible things to a man just out the clink. What's done's done, I figured. But now I see's the truth. Now I'se see I should'a tole ya 'mediately,' cos you gotta right ta know what went on fer real."

"I'se 'preciate it, Grandpap, an' I'se understand. An' I'se love ya fer it," Travis said, liftin' the bucket pole ta take down the creek. An' then he left, he did. An' while's he were trudgin' down the creek, he couldn't help but 'member what

69

his grandaddy tole him last night, an' what were worse was that he couldn't do nothing 'bout it. Caudill's two boys was dead, one'a the fudge-packer disease, an' the other'a hippie drugger, and Caudill hisself were now livin' up'n a big fancy mansion in Pulaski, an' Pulsaki were so far, his grandpap's truck wouldn't get there halfways 'fore it throwed a rod or busted the crankshaft. So Travis felt mighty useless indeed, an' as he trundled those buckets down the creek, he closed his eyes an' fairly prayed:

God, I knows full well I ain't been much of a worthy servant, an' I'se heart-lee sorry fer my worldly sins, but— holy ever-livin'-shit, God!—if You on high'd give me the chance ta get my proper revenge fer what the Caudills done ta my fine paw an' lovin' maw, I swears to ya, I'd be a better servant to you an' yer holy needs, I would!

An', wouldn't ya know it! It wouldn't be more'n 15 minutes 'fore God Hisself'd answered Travis Clyde Tuckton's prayers.

* * *

Grandpap kept'a bangin' out those soleprints, hand made each an' ever one. Was hard work, but hard work made men good, he'd heard. So's he's was sittin' there in his wheelchair, workin' on his fine boots an' shoes, when the door done swunged open.

An' in the doorway, backed by the grand sunlight, he were standin' there, his Rolls Royce viserble behind him in the dirt drive.

It were Thibald Caudill.

"Hey, ol' pappy," he greeted, all's decked up in his citified charcoal-gray suit an' queer Eye-talian shoes. "'Member me? I'se bet'cha do."

"Thibald Caudill," Grandpappy acknowledged, seethin' on the inside, an' tremorin' in his gut. "Why's *you* here?"

"Ever now an' then, I like ta drives 'round the old homestead, ya know? Ta shows me where I comes from. So's I thought I'd drop by."

"Ain't no reason fer ya ta drop by here, Caudill," Grandpappy croaked.

"Aw, shee-it, Grandpappy Martin!" Caudill, then throwed his head back an' laughed, he did, the sun glarin' offa his mostly bald head with gray tricklin' down his ears. "I see's ya still got yer dander up on account'a that foolhearty story 'bout me'n my boys killin' yer kin. Shee-it! Ain't no truth ta that, Pappy! My word!"

Yer word, Thibald Caudill, ain't worth two squirts'a piss from a dead dog's dick, Grandpappy thought.

"So's let's put alls that behind us, huh, pappy? Seein' that yer an inverlid now, what with no feet, I figured I'd come up here an' make a deal. See's, I gots me a fair load'a yardhands, pick my weeds, mow my lawn an' the like, an' theys all need new boots, good 'uns, an' I'se figured you still make those fine handstitched workboots like ya used ta. So's that's why I'se up here." Caudill reached inta his pocket an' withdrew a right fat wad'a bills. "I got's six yardhands, I do, an' I figures boots as good as yours ain't gonna come cheap, so's I'll take six pair fer a hunnert dollars'a pair. How's that, ol' man?"

Caudill slapped the money down. It were a right lotta money, it was, but Grandpap felt it'd be a gross injustice ta take green cash from the same man who kilt his daughter'n son'n law, so's he said instead, "Take yer fuckin' money an' yer devil-butt-lickin' self outa here, Thibald Caudill, 'fore I'se up an' kill ya!"

Caudill chuckled. "Who? *You,* ol' man? Beat me ta death with those stinky stumps ya got where yer feet should be?" An' then Caudill throwed his head back agin, an' let loose with a fresh burst'a laughter so loud it'd probably wake up half the folks layin' in Beall Cemetery.

It were mighty embarrassin', it were, fer Grandpappy, ta have this rube walkin' inta his home an' makin' a mockery of him. But, lo, there weren't nothin' Grandpap could do, not confined ta the blasted chair an' with no feet!

"Yeah, I'll'se bet'cher still humpin' dogs, ya old cracker, huh? So poor out here ya probably got's ta blow yer nose in yer hand whenever ya git hungry? Ain't gots nothin' but crusty sticks fer feet, ain't got no life 'cept ta sit here starin' at the wall. Why don't'cha do the world a favor, ol' coot, an' dig yerself a big hole an' buries yerself?"

Caudill's fat face gleamed in the sunlight, an' turnt fairly pink from the next round'a laughter. An' ol' Grandpap Martin, right then he could'a put a gun ta his head was how low and disgraced he felt. But then—

Then—

Then front door swang open.

An' it were Travis who walked in.

* * *

Cummings parked in a wooded dell just off of the old Governor's Bridge. Just after noon. Gloved, now, he very carefully wiped down each bag of cocaine with isopropanol to eradicate his prints in the event anyone found the empty bags. Then he slit each bag—all 10 of them—and dumped them over the side, where they splashed gently into the burbling creek below. *There's going to be some high fish in Russell County today,* he thought. Keeping the cocaine would've defied even his ethics. Even if he did have a way to sell it, he didn't want to contribute any more to the denigration of America. The money would be enough. And killing Spaz and Dutch?

Fuck them, he rationalized. *They were drug dealers.*

Next, he knew, he'd have to stash the money, give that fire he'd set, as well as its potential consequences, plenty of time to cool off. He wasn't too keen on the idea of driving around in a federal police car with a trunk full of $100 bills. But where could he make the stash?

The sky, bright, cloudless, gorgeous, beckoned him. He pulled out of the dell and eventually cruised back to the Route. The afterimage of what he'd done remained surprisingly neutral. *Killed two guys, burned a shack, dumped 10 keys in the drink, and walked with enough cash to fix the county deficit.* Cummings shrugged. But it was all for something more important, wasn't it? It was for Kath. It was for the kind of life she deserved. And those two dealers? The world wouldn't likely miss them.

He pulled over around the next bend; a girl in ragtag clothes was limping along the shoulder. A hill girl. *Give her a ride,* he thought. It was easy to be charitable when you had a bag of c-notes in your trunk.

"Howdy," she said. "Thanks much."

"No problem."

"I'se—" Then she stalled. The car, true, was unmarked, but Cummings himself wasn't, not in his navy-blue police tunic and gold badge, and not with a gunbelt around his waist. "Relax," he said. "I'm not looking to hassle anyone."

You're ATF, ain't ya?" she said.

"That's right."

She fell silent. Of course. She probably had relatives who ran moonshine. *I'm the big bad government,* he realized. *To her, I'm the guy who makes her life that much harder.*

"Where you headed?"

"Up near Filbert."

"No problem."

He cruised on, over long rolling roads, side-eyed her once or twice. A pretty little girl, 16 probably, ample bosomed. A trace scent of sweat hovered off her, something Cummings had grown used to. She was a stereotype sitting right next to him: the barefoot hillgirl, lank dark hair flecked with straw, peevish, unbra'd beneath the thread-bare sundress.

"Pretty day."

"Shore is."

"Let me ask you something," he said, finally remembering his talk with Jan Beck. *You got a couple hundred grand in the trunk, try earning your pay today, Stew.* "You ever heard of a guy named Travis Clyde Tuckton?"

"Oh, shore. Nice fella 'fore he went up ta the county prison. Never knowed him well, but he were nice." Her hair, now, was a brunet tumult in the open-windowed breeze. Plain, pretty. A simple girl with fine hair under her arms. "He's still up there."

No, he's not, honey. He got out, skipped his parole, and

now he's . . . fucking people's brains. Nice fella?

"Well, I heard his folks got killed, and his house burned down," Cummings tried to bait her.

"Yeah," was all she replied.

"Well, Travis got released recently, and with his house burned down, where would he go?"

Her eyes narrowed. Her hands lay in her lap like small white birds. "He in trouble agin?"

"No, no, nothing like that. State tax office owes him money, that's all. Like to know where he's staying, so he can get his proper refund."

"Oh, well," she spoke right up at the lie. "I doubt he'd come back here. This county's dead."

"Yeah, you're probably right. But if he *did* come back here, where would he go?"

She brushed hair out of her eyes, picked out a strand of straw. Cummings couldn't help but notice the high, full breasts, and the nipples distending through sweat-moist cotton. "Well, he's got a grandpap on his mama's side, Jake Martin. But he's problee dead b'now. He was old, an' he didn't have no feet, doctor hadda cut 'em off like 'bout over five years ago on account of some disease. Hadda ol' cottage up the woods offa the ol' Tick Neck."

Tick Neck Road, Cummings thought. South county. He'd heard of it, just had never been up there. *Lost his feet? Probably diabetes-related gangrene, and she's right. He's probably dead.* Hill folk didn't go to doctors much. Cummings was pissing into the wind.

"Here's your stop," he said and pulled over at the crossroads. The sky opened bright and blue before him. A swarm of birds passed.

"Thanks much," she repeated, opening the door.

"Sure—hey, wait." There *was* something else he could ask, wasn't there? The plaster casts. A sole imprint that wasn't indexed in the state computer. *Handmade boots,* Jan Beck had posited.

The girl remained leaned over, fresh cleavage like a beacon. There was something pleasant or even erotic about

74

the faint sweat-scent.

"You know anyone around here who makes boots, shoes, leather gear?" he asked.

Her bland face pinched up in some perplexion. "Well, yeah, an' that's a might funny ya asked."

"Why?"

"On account of what'cha asked before."

"I don't get it," Cummings admitted.

Her face seemed to float before the sky. "See, there was a fella who made boots 'round here, fine boots they was, an' it's the same fella I'se just told ya 'bout. Jake Martin. Travis Tuckton's grandpap."

* * *

She'd given directions, at least to the best of his comprehension. The information put a fast spark in him. *Yeah, this Jake Martin, he's probably dead, state cops've probably already checked it out, but—*

Header, the word came like a spirit's voice. *Head-humpin'.*

Cummings had more important things to worry about now, like where to secret a veritable shitload of bands of $100 bills that he'd ripped off of a drug dealer he'd murdered. But the case—this bizarre, inexplicable set of sexual homicides—had long-since put a hook in him. At the very least, it couldn't hurt to look into the loke.

Off Tick Neck, he thought. He was there now, cruising slowly up the road's winding cant. There were a lot of side roads, but . . .

No mail routes, no addresses. Anybody who lived back here wasn't a legally censused resident. These roads had no street names, some of them weren't even on the county map grid.

Cain't's remember too good, the girl had told him just before she'd left. *But I'se think ya turn 'cross from the deadfall, the big 'un. You'll's see it . . .*

Just when Cummings would give up, there it was: a

75

deadfall of logs, branches, and cut brambles. The county left them all the time after storms, but this one, Cummings noted, was large as it was old. Rotten and falling in on itself. He veered left up a dirt-scratch lane barely wide enough to admit the car.

Wound up and around. And—

Wham.

A cottage, just like the girl had said. Ramshackle old place, falling in on itself like the deadfall. Ivy growing up rotted sideboarding, missing shingles like missing teeth. A human pock in the woods. But—

What the fuck?

This was the craziest thing he'd ever seen. A squatter cottage, yes, but parked right before the crumbling front porch sat a gleaming Rolls Royce Silver Shadow.

Guess this old man Martin's not dead after all, Cummings assumed, but the rest was folly. *A hillfolk shoemaker? Must sell a lot of shoes to be able to drive a car like that . . .*

Cummings pulled right up. If he wanted the element of surprise, he'd blown it royally; anyone in the cottage would be able to hear his car ease up. But, wait—

No, he thought.

They wouldn't be able to hear at all. Because another sound permeated the surrounding woods.

A high-pitched screech.

A . . . Cummings' ponderings were guillotined by what he next thought. It couldn't be. No cop was that lucky.

The screech sounded like a power tool. A power *drill.*

No way, no way, he thought. He disembarked, walked up to the house, peeked into a side window.

Cramped room. Would've been large were it not for all the junk. Tools, leather sheets hanging. Rows and rows of hand-carved wooden shoeblocks. And—

A table.

No . . . way, but this time the thought was drained as a bled pig.

The screeching ceased. Then a voice erupted, a crotchety, old hillbilly voice.

"Get it, son. Ooo-eee! Cut yerself a *good* peckerhole in that cracker head! I ain't lyin' ta ya, Travis! This here's the white trash bastard who done head-humped yer maw!"

Was Cummings gazing into a rent in hell? On the table lay a well-dressed man, on his back, a cleanly cut hole gushing blood as a ham-hock hand withdrew a knife from the hole. The hand belonged to Travis Clyde Tuckton, the boy whose photograph Cummings had already seen at the state crime lab. And sitting off from the table was a wizened, whiskered old man in a wheelchair. A man with—

No feet, Cummings recognized.

Jake Martin. Tuckton's grandfather . . .

"I'se so pissed, I'se in a *swivet,* Grandpap!"

"Only fittin' an' proper, son. Just like it says in God's book. An eye fer a eye!"

"An' a head fer a head!"

Cummings stared.

The boy, a big, brawny, short-haired lad with a surprisingly friendly face, lowered his trousers and promptly inserted his erect penis into the hole in the corpse's head. Then, biting his lower lip in a perverse rage, he grabbed the corpse's ears, and—

Began to hump.

He began to hump the head.

"Ooo-eee!" the footless old man exclaimed. "Hump that there evil head, boy, I say, *hump* it!"

As Cummings stared on, his sentience felt akin to a swamp rat racing round in his mind, madly seeking exit. The old man in the chair had his penis out too, was masturbating as he whooped. And Tuckton continued to hump the head in a fury . . .

"Yeah, Travis! Do'm up *reeeeeal* good!" the old man celebrated, his hand choking his own penis like a chicken neck. "Get'cher self off a *dandy* nut in that there head!"

"Gonna come in his head so hard, Grandpappy," the boy huffed, humping away, "my peckersnot's gonna squirt out his butt!"

"Yeah, boy! Yeeeeeah!"

77

So here it was, right before Cummings' eyes. He'd stumbled upon this, he was *watching* it, for God's sake. He was bearing witness to the same macabre crime which had obsessed him for months.

He was witnessing a header . . .

Cummings, an automaton now, unholstered his service revolver. Turned. Walked up the porch steps and entered the dilapidated house.

"Aw, shee-it, Grandpap," he heard. "I'se gonna gets me off my first nut likes *real fast* in this cracker head!"

"Go fer it, boy! Get it! We'se got all night ta fuck that head, plenty time fer more nuts. Why, I'se'll hump four 'er five times myself! So don't'cha worry 'bout comin' fast. Pipe a load a juice that'd make yer daddy *proud!*"

Numb, and oddly fearless, Cummings stepped into the room.

"Who the *hail!*" the old man cracked.

The boy, evidently in the spasms of orgasm, slowed down his pelvic thrusts into the corpse-head and opened his eyes.

"'S'a cop!" he realized.

BAM!

Cummings squeezed off the first shot. The boy's eye disappeared as a pulpy red blur, and he fell away from the table, from the . . . head. He landed on the wood floor hard as a side of fresh-butchered beef, his erection still pulsing down, offering semen to the air.

"Ya blammed fuckin' cop! Look what'cha done!"

BAM!

Cummings' second shot caught the old man in the belly, who doubled over in the wheelchair. And—

BAM!

The third shot divided the top of his head almost as cleanly as a machete through a melon.

Cummings stood. Stared. For the second time in a day his eyes went wide in spite of rising cordite. Silence like a graveyard at 3 a.m. insinuated about him, and so did the simple thought.

I just solved the head-humping murders.

That's all it had taken. Three shots from his service revolver, and it was all over . . .

What . . . now? There was no phone, no way to report the incident to the state. And on this side of the ridge, his radio probably wouldn't reach the dispatcher.

Leave the house. Take the evidence. Go back to the FO and report to State, he thought robotically.

And Cummings did just that. He redonned his gloves, grabbed a cardboard box from a random shelf. He took a boot off the body of Travis Clyde Tuckton, grabbed the power-drill still fitted with the 3-inch holesaw, grabbed the kitchen knife, and put it all in the box. Then he took it all out to the car and drove back to the Russell County BATF Field Office.

* * *

The drive back left him stunned—or, not so much the drive, but his musings. Talk about a busy day. *I killed four men in a handful of hours,* he reminded himself at the wheel. The Route opened up, passed endless cornfields and slat-gapped barns. But only two of the dead men mattered. Tuckton and Martin.

The head-humpers.

It was a revitalization he needed. Killing two drug dealers and copping their green was one thing. But . . . this? In a matter of minutes, and with three shots from his duty piece, he'd solved a murder case . . .

Cummings parked. A state unmarked was in the lot too, and he could only guess that they were following up Beck's evidence, talking to Peerce. *Save your breath, boys,* he thought proudly. *I just solved the case.* The grotesquerie of what he'd seen was far behind him. He could deal with that later.

He walked into the FO.

"I did it, boss," he announced.

Peerce looked up from his desk.

Cummings was nearly out of breath now. "I solved the

head-humping murders."

"Ya did . . . *what?*"

"Caught them in the act, saw it with my own eyes. Shot them. They were . . . doing it right there in the window."

"Stew—"

"Ex-con named Tuckton, and his grandfather. Had some guy right there on the table and they were . . . humping . . . his head."

"Stew, shut up a minute."

Cummings peered. "What's wrong, J.L.? I just got done telling you I solved the header murders."

Peerce spat in his proverbial cup. Only then did Cummings notice the other man in the claustrophobic office.

Hard-looking guy, tall. State uniform but he had stripes down his pants and a crest on the bill of his hat. A state captain or above . . .

But Cummings noticed something else.

The state officer had his gun drawn.

"This here's Major Phil Straker," Peerce told him. "He's liaison officer 'tween state IAD an' narcotics."

"Narc—" But that's all Cummings could get out.

"Yer unner arrest, Stew, fer two count's'a first degree murder."

Cummings felt bolted in place.

"Not to mention," this Straker added, "obstruction of justice, complicity with known felonious criminals, misprision of a felony, the willful theft of ill-gotten gains, and possession and illegal transport of controlled dangerous substances."

"Don't even say nothin', Stew. They got'cha cold," Peerce said. On his desk was a portable field VCR. Peerce turned it on, toned up the tiny screen.

My God, Cummings thought.

There, right there on the screen, Cummings saw himself, placing first the gym bag and then 10 bags of cocaine into the trunk of his federal car . . .

"That's *two* counts of murder, Agent Cummings," Straker spoke up again, "but one of the men you murdered was a state police officer."

"Dutch," Cummings murmured.

"That's right. He was a state narcotics plant working a sting. We had cameras inside and one outside, for tag numbers. The cameras inside, of course, burned up in the fire you set. But the one outside . . ."

Straker's free hand bid the VCR screen. On it, Cummings was driving away.

"You're fucked, Stew," Peerce said. "You're a asshole."

"The murder of a police officer," Straker was kind enough to embellish, "as you probably know, carries a mandatory sentence of death in this state."

I'm caught, Cummings thought simply. *I'm dead.*

But he wasn't dead yet, was he?

"Stew, unholster yer piece an' set it on my desk. *Real slow like.*"

Straker had his own piece on him. *I'm not going down,* Cummings thought. *I'd rather punch out now than spend a decade getting butt-fucked in the can while my appeals run out.*

Cummings, very slowly, set his service revolver on Peerce's desk.

"Good boy," Straker said.

Cummings shrugged, then, in an instant, lashed his hands out, remembering the pistol-disarm technique they'd taught him in the Army. His hands wrapped around Straker's gun, pushed away—

BAM!

The bullet grazed his side but he didn't even feel it.

"Goddamn it, Stew, don't'cha even—"

The automaton again, Cummings had disarmed Straker in less than one full second, had the guy's piece in his hand.

Straker, though shit-scared, tried to maintain his authority. "Don't be stupid, Cummings. You can plea-bargain your way out maybe. You can say you killed them in self-defense and were bringing the money and the coke back here. But if you kill us, you're finished."

BAM!

BAM-BAM!

He took out Peerce first, a clean headshot, then punched Straker's ticket with a double-tap in the 5x, a heartshot. Blood jetted out of the holes a good three feet. Peerce lay limp in his office chair, the back of his head emptied. Brown tobacco juice drooled as a single rope from the corner of his mouth.

Cummings head was ticking; the swamp rat was back, whipping more circles, trying to find a way out.

Be cool, he ordered himself, though that was not particularly easy considering he'd killed six men today, three of them police officers. *What's done is done. Don't freak out. Think.*

Plea bargain? No way. He'd already dumped the cocaine. No judge would buy it. He'd done the only thing he could do to preserve his own life. The way he saw it, he had maybe an hour lead before anyone found the bodies, more if he was lucky. He'd have to pinch a car, blow over the state line, then steal more cars along the way till he got to Mexico. There was no other way.

After all, he still had all that money in his trunk.

Out of here.

He didn't even take a final look around. He left the VCR; surely Straker wasn't the only state narc who'd seen the surveillance tape. So he got into his car and drove.

Best to stay off the interstate. They'd have an APB out on his car soon, so he'd have to steal something quick, and abduct the owner so the car wouldn't be reported stolen. Who knew? But—

What am I doing? He decelerated, then pulled a U.

Kath . . .

He couldn't just disappear. He owed her an explanation, at least. And the money? He'd leave her half, to keep her on her feet and pay her pharmacy bills. Hell, even half of the cash, U.S. greenbacks, would last a long time in Mexico. But it wasn't just that—

I've got to—Suddenly Cummings, a cold-blooded murderer, a *cop* killer, was in tears.

82

I've got to see her one last time . . .

In one afternoon he'd destroyed his entire life. And the only *good* thing that remained in that life was Kath. *My God. What have I done?*

There could be no point in deliberating regrets, no logic in reconsideration. It was a cruel world, and sometimes people had to do cruel things. Ripping off the money, killing Dutch and Spaz? It was either that or live in squalor, weighed down by Kath's medical bills. They both deserved better than that. All he wanted was enough to get by. It was the chance he had to take, and the whole thing went sour. From the beginning, he'd never had a choice.

Dust followed him up the gravel road to his house. He skidded to a halt. In a waking nightmare, he saw a house full of State SWAT and DEA tac men, waiting for him, waiting for the cop killer. But the house was pin-drop silent when he entered. No shadows in wait.

Gym bag in tow, he walked down the dim hall to the bedroom. She was probably resting, worn out by the fatigue of her illness. What would she say? How would she react? Cummings brushed aside tears, his hand on the doorknob. Disgusted with him? Appalled? *All that and more,* he realized.

He could just leave half of the money, then drive away, call her later. Anything not to have to face her with what he'd done. But that wouldn't work, either. By then the state would be tracing any incoming calls. He'd be caught.

Be a man, you asshole. Go in, wake her up, and tell her.

The gym bag felt as heavy as a bag full of body parts, or dead babies. The door stood slightly ajar. But just before he could open it, he heard—

"Yeah, like that."

Kath's voice.

She must be on the phone, he discerned. Then paranoia kicked in. Had the state called her? Were they talking to her right now, rubbing the revelation in her face that her husband was a murderer? But no, that couldn't be. Her voice sounded normal, even enlivened.

"Want more?"

Cummings' brow furrowed. Then he heard another voice. A man's.

"Yeah, cut me another line."

Cummings peeked in the gap, and that was when the rest of his world collapsed.

Kath lay naked on the bed, spread-legged and grinning. She was giggling as a naked man—Dr. Seymour, no less—inhaled lines of cocaine off her belly, simultaneously rubbing the furred plot of her sex.

"Where do you *get* this good blow, Jimmy?" she asked.

The pharmacist leaned up, wiped white power off his nose. "I got my sources." Then he chuckled, his finger still in the groove of Kath's vagina. "Bet your husband'd shit a brick if he knew."

Kath laughed. Her sweaty face looked aglow in untold delights. "Are you kidding? He'd kill us both!"

"It's amazing how stupid he is, though." Now the man was rubbing her breasts, so nonchalant. "Just keeps forking over the cash week after week, and never suspects a thing."

"I'm a good actress, Jimmy. The asshole still thinks I'm so sick I'm about to die. And he believes it all because I show him those phony doctor slips and drug prescriptions you give me. He thinks I'm using all that money for medicine!"

"Yeah, well this is some fine medicine," the man said, shaking the bag of white powder.

"And he just got a raise!"

They both laughed like jackals, Kath's breasts bobbing. Cummings could only stand there and watch, as if anodized, as if the truth had reverted him to a six-foot block of cement.

"Come on, let's do it again," Kath purred, cupping the man's genitals. "Stew doesn't get home till six."

"Christ, Kath! I done come in ya twice already. Give a guy a chance to get it up again!"

"You'll get it up," she assured, "and when you do, I want it up the ass."

"Aw, shit, aw, Christ, honey, you sure know how to suck a cock."

84

What the universe was now treating Cummings to, of course, was the witness of his wife performing expert fellatio on this Jimmy, the town general practitioner, who lay back in Cummings bed with his eyes closed.

And, next—

The swamp rat stopped.

When the doctor opened his eyes, though, Cummings' gun was in his face. The face drained. The mouth opened to speak.

BAM!

Kath's head rose, her naked body bucked. She screamed. Jimmy's head emptied glistening brains on the pillow.

"Stew!" Kath shrieked, turning in a blur of flesh. "I—"

BAM! BAM!

She lay back howling.

"Just to make sure you don't go anywhere," Cummings said, reholstering his Smith. No, he hadn't killed her. He'd blown out her kneecaps.

Then he walked out of the house and put the gym bag back in the trunk.

Yes, it was a cruel world indeed, and it was about to get a little bit crueller.

From the trunk he retrieved the box he'd taken out of the old man's cottage, the box containing the evidence: the power drill, the knife, and the hole-saw bit.

Cummings' gaze turned to the sky. It was a beautiful day. He lit a Lucky, dragged, and let the smoke eddy from his mouth. Then he grabbed the box.

It was a short walk back to the house.

85

AFTERWORD

"Header."

"We'se havin' a header tonight, yessir!"

"Hump that head, boy! I say HUMP it!"

These are the mighty peculiar lines of dialogue that slammed unbidden into my mind some time in the early '90s when, after having been lucky enough to sell several mass-market paperbacks, I had become apprized of an alternate avenue in the horror genre called the "small press ." See, it was occurring to me that, as much as I enjoyed writing novels for companies like Zebra/Pinnacle and Berkley/Diamond, it would be cool to be able to write–and to sell–horror fiction that crossed the tradition boundaries that existed in the mass-market. Uncut. Uncensored. No holds barred.

Down and dirty and deep in the gutter.

Why?

Because, I guess, there's an aspect of my creative brain that very much wallows in that self-same gutter.

By this time, I was beginning to actualize my infatuation (and sequent FEAR) of rednecks. My first novel *Ghouls* had rednecks in it, and one of my very first short stories, "The Man Who Loved Cliches," revolved around a very unlikely redneck antagonist. (It wasn't a very good story, but that's beside the point.) At the same time, Dave Barnett was putting out a daring and very cool small-press mag called *Into The Darkness*, a mag that purported to attend to horror fiction that crossed previously mentioned boundaries, and he was kind enough to publish a favorite early piece of mine called "The Wrong Guy." (This story entailed, in unrestrained detail, female-to-male rape, live-snake enemas, gun-brush urinary catheters, live penis dissection, and the like. Not your typical fare, in other words.) Hence, and to my creative jubilation, here was my gutter-brain outlet!

87

Simultaneously, Dave had mentioned that he was thinking of publishing books and chapbooks. Now, I'm too friggin' OLD to remember the exact chronology (Dave, for instance, via his book imprint Necro Publications, would later publish my hardcore nihilistic porn/horror novel *The Bighead* and my collaborative hardcore smut/wrestling novella that I wrote with John Pelan, *Goon*). But during this time, my gutter-brain was brewing many, many unsavory things, including the three lines of less-than-seemly dialogue that begin this Afterword. Given my inexplicable infatuation/loathe of rednecks, I was becoming obsessed with the idea of writing a novella that incorporated the age-old Crazy Screaming Rednecks In The Woods formula, but then did something a little much with it. Something that hadn't been done before.

Humpin' heads, is what I'm talkin' about. You know. Cuttin' yerself a hole in a fella or a gal's coconut and then gettin' yer willy up in that there brain and, you know...

Humpin' that head.

Seems a little much to me. Seems different. Something that–to my knowledge, at least–has never occurred in a piece of fiction before. Damn it, I wanted to do it! (Write the story, I mean, not hump a head.) Perhaps the bedrock for this peculiar creative endeavor has its provenance in the just-as-age-old military training invective "I'll pop your eyeball out and SKULL-fuck you!" an invective which anyone who's been in the military was threatened with by upstanding drill sergeants. The actuality of this process, however, seemed flawed. You can't pop somebody's eyeball out and then, well, you know. The inner rim of the outer eyesocket is hardly large enough and, secondly, you'd have to remove the entire back of the ocular cavity. Just didn't seem right to me. Ah, but if you had a "hole-saw" on the end of a power drill?

Hence, *Header*.

Would Dave Barnett actually publish such a thing if I indeed took the time to write it? Well, write it, I did, and publish it, he did.

For this I'm am very, very grateful. Because, Necro's chapbook release of *Header* comprised the very beginning of my love-affair with over-the-top, uncensored small-press horror. The first edition of *Header* (a simple scarlet, softcovered, stapled chap) and its second printing in my hardcover Necro novella collection *Sex, Drugs, & Power Tools* remain to this day considerable collector's items. But it is due to this first chap that I still enjoy a presence in the wonderful world of small-press extreme horror. I dig that presence to no end. Thank you, Dave.

Later in the '90s, thanks to a generous tip from the brilliant novelist Rex Miller, I was able to sell several comic scripts to Glenn Danzig for publication in his eye-popping and penultimate comic line, Verotika. When Glenn's editorial manager asked me to script *Header*, I almost keeled over. "Holy shit!" I thought. "These folks want to make a COMIC out of my novella about rednecks humpin' heads!" I could scarcely comprehend this–evidently, they had to speak to a lawyer first–but, Gawd dang it, I wrote the script, sent it in, and it got published in glorious color and looked great. In fact, Glenn Danzig's Verotika, Inc., published five scripts by me, *Header* among them, and he paid pro rates at a time when I sorely needed the dough. I couldn't begin to thank Glenn enough for his support of my work. It would be an impossibility.

Many novels and several years later, Overlook Connection owner, Dave Hinchberger, passed on an inquiry from a fan named Michael Kennedy (since I didn't, and quite foolishly, STILL don't have an official website with a proper contact on it.) But Michael Kennedy made to me the strangest proposal . . .

He wanted to make *Header* into a movie.

Well, somehow, I didn't believe it. The prospect was . . . incogitable, as H.P. Lovecraft might say. No way anyone was crazy enough to make a movie about rednecks gettin' it on with . . . heads. I figured he was mentally ill or something. But in my business, there's this unwritten edict: "No matter how crazy they sound, never say no until you see if their money's green." I kept this edict to heart and, believe it or not, Kennedy and his associate Mike Anthony (a Yankees fan, no less–God bless him) actually came all the way to Florida to visit me and buy me dinner and beers. They didn't seem mentally ill. And later in the evening we went to–yes!–a redneck bar, and these guys whipped out a "film prospectus" detailing the film's entire budget, shooting schedule, investor offerings, etc. It looked very squared away, and these two guys seemed squared away as well; in fact . . . more squared away then me. I signed on the dotted line, and at the following Horrorfind Convention, Kennedy and Anthony gave me MONEY.

And it was green.

To make a long Afterword short, *Header* was filmed in upstate New York during the summer of (shit, I can't remember, 2003, I think.) Kennedy and Anthony even flew me and my pal Jack Ketchum to the location and let us have speaking roles in the movie. (I didn't botch my lines, so I knew that was a good omen.) The rest, in a sense, is an oddment of history. My first hardcore novella became my first comic and my first movie. And you wanna know the best part?

The movie kicks ass.

Thank you for buying this rather long-awaited reprint of *Header*. It's near and dear to me. My career has been a wonderful excursion that's so much fun I surely don't deserve it, and more than anything else, *Header* is the reason I've been able to undertake that excursion. The excursion goes on, mind you, something else I'm very, very grateful for. Specifically, I must thank Dave Barnett, Glenn Danzig, Michael Kennedy, and Mike Anthony, but I must also thank the entire cast and crew of the movie, and also Jerry Chandler and Don May at Synapse Films; also Thomas Deja, Tony Timpone, and Mike Gingold at Fangoria. First and foremost, however, I must bestow unbridled gratitude to my fans, namely you. Thank you.

I hope you enjoyed *Header*.

Edward Lee
Somewhere in northern Florida at about 33,000 feet
May 10, 2011

ABOUT THE AUTHOR

Edward Lee has authored close to 50 books in the field of horror; he specializes in hardcore fare. His most recent novels are LUCIFER'S LOTTERY and the Lovecraftian THE HAUNTER OF THE THRESHOLD. His movie HEADER was released on DVD by Synapse Film in June, 2009. Lee lives in Largo, Florida.

YOU'VE READ THE BOOK
NOW SEE THE DISTURBING MOVIE

"One of the most over-the-top horror films I've seen in a long time."
—Tony Timpone, *Fangoria Magazine*

"One of the most appalling, sexually depraved, downright disgustingly enjoyable independent films I have ever seen."
—Dreadcentral.com

"Easily one of the most fucked up movies I have ever seen."
—Brad Miska, Editor in Chief of *Bloody-Disgusting*

"Sure to become a cult classic."
—Feoamante.com

"It's a ferociously engaging flick and damned well made to boot . . . Header *has got to be seen!"*
—Joblo.com

*"[*Header*] carves out a filthy niche all its own, with a subject matter so utterly taboo that you can barely believe what's before you;"* and *"to create a motion picture that is more graphic, perverse, depraved, and amoral will be a very tough feat indeed"*
—Mark Lee, *DVD Times.com*

*"*Header *is one helluva twisted, gory movie. You may not be the same after you have watched it."*
—Popsyndicate.com

**Visit
ww.WhatsAHeader.com
for more details**

deadite
press

"Brain Cheese Buffet" Edward Lee - collecting nine of Lee's most sought after tales of violence and body fluids. Featuring the Stoker nominated "Mr. Torso," the legendary gross-out piece "The Dritiphilist," the notorious "The McCrath Model SS40-C, Series S," and six more stories to test your gag reflex.
"Edward Lee's writing is fast and mean as a chain saw revved to full-tilt boogie."
   - Jack Ketchum

"Bullet Through Your Face" Edward Lee - No writer is more extreme, perverted, or gross than Edward Lee. His world is one of psychopathic redneck rapists, sex addicted demons. and semen stealing aliens. Brace yourself, the king of splatterspunk is guaranteed to shock, offend, and make you laugh until you vomit.
"Lee pulls no purches."
   - Fangoria

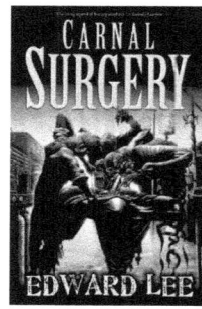

"Carnal Surgery" Edward Lee - Autopsy fetishes, crippled sex slaves, a serial killer who keeps the hands of his victims, government conspiracies, dead cops and doomed pornographers. From operating room morality plays to a town that serves up piss and cum mixed drinks, this is the strange and disturbing world of Edward Lee. From one of the most notorious, controversial, and extreme voices in horror fiction comes a new collection of depravity and terror. Carnal Surgery collects eleven of Lee's most sought after tales of sex and dismemberment.

"Trolley No. 1852" Edward Lee - In 1934, horror writer H.P. Lovecraft is invited to write a story for a subversive underground magazine, all on the condition that a pseudonym will be used. The pay is lofty, and God knows, Lovecraft needs the money. There's just one catch. It has to be a pornographic story . . . The 1852 Club is a bordello unlike any other. Its women are the most beautiful and they will do anything. But there is something else going on at this sex club. In the back rooms monsters are performing vile acts on each other and doors to other dimensions are opening . . .

"The Haunter of the Threshold" Edward Lee - There is something very wrong with this backwater town. Suicide notes, magic gems, and haunted cabins await her. Plus the woods are filled with monsters, both human and otherworldly. And then there are the horrible tentacles . . . Soon Hazel is thrown into a battle for her life that will test her sanity and sex drive. The sequel to H.P. Lovecraft's The Haunter of the Dark is Edward Lee's most pornographic novel to date!

"The Innswich Horror" Edward Lee - In July, 1939, antiquarian and H.P. Lovecraft aficionado, Foster Morley, takes a scenic bus tour through northern Massachusetts and finds Innswich Point. There far too many similarities between this fishing village and the fictional town of Lovecraft's masterpiece, The Shadow Over Innsmouth. Join splatter king Edward Lee for a private tour of Innswich Point - a town founded on perversion, torture, and abominations from the sea.

"Mangled Meat" Edward Lee - No writer is more hardcore, offensive, or notorious than Edward Lee. His world is one of torture, bizarre fetishes, and alien autopsies. Prepare yourself, as these three novellas from the king of splatterspunk are guaranteed to make you gasp, gag, and laugh your ass off. Featuring The Decortication Technician, The Cyesolagniac and Room 415.

"All You Can Eat" Shane McKenzie - Deep in Texas there is a Chinese restaurant that harbors a secret. Its food is delicious and the secret ingredient ensures that once you have one bite you'll never be able to stop. But when the food runs out and the customers turn to cannibalism, the kitchen staff must take up arms against these obese people-eaters or else be next on the menu!

THE VERY BEST IN CULT HORROR

deadite
press

"Genital Grinder" Ryan Harding - *"Think you're hardcore? Think again. If you've handled everything Edward Lee, Wrath James White, and Bryan Smith have thrown at you, then put on your rubber parka, spread some plastic across the floor, and get ready for Ryan Harding, the unsung master of hardcore horror. Abandon all hope, ye who enter here. Harding's work is like an acid bath, and pain has never been so sweet."*
- Brian Keene

"Ghoul" Brian Keene - There is something in the local cemetery that comes out at night. Something that is unearthing corpses and killing people. It's the summer of 1984 and Timmy and his friends are looking forward to no school, comic books, and adventure. But instead they will be fighting for their lives. The ghoul has smelled their blood and it is after them. But that's not the only monster they will face this summer . . . From award-winning horror master Brian Keene comes a novel of monsters, murder, and the loss of innocence.

"Clickers" J. F. Gonzalez and Mark Williams- They are the Clickers, giant venomous blood-thirsty crabs from the depths of the sea. The only warning to their rampage of dismemberment and death is the terrible clicking of their claws. But these monsters aren't merely here to ravage and pillage. They are being driven onto land by fear. Something is hunting the Clickers. Something ancient and without mercy. *Clickers* is J. F. Gonzalez and Mark Williams' gore-soaked cult classic tribute to the giant monster B-movies of yesteryear.

"Clickers II" J. F. Gonzalez and Brian Keene- Thousands of Clickers swarm across the entire nation and march inland, slaughtering anyone and anything they come across. But this time the Clickers aren't blindly rushing onto land - they are being led by an intelligence older than civilization itself. A force that wants to take dry land away from the mammals. Those left alive soon realize that they must do everything and anything they can to protect humanity – no matter the cost. *This isn't war, this is extermination.*

"Jack's Magic Beans" Brian Keene - It happens in a split-second. One moment, customers are happily shopping in the Save-A-Lot grocery store. The next instant, they are transformed into bloodthirsty psychotics, interested only in slaughtering one another and committing unimaginably atrocious and frenzied acts of violent depravity. Deadite Press is proud to bring one of Brian Keene's bleakest and most violent novellas back into print once more. This edition also includes four bonus short stories:

"Whargoul" Dave Brockie - It is a beast born in bullets and shrapnel, feeding off of pain, misery, and hard drugs. Cursed to wander the Earth without the hope of death, it is reborn again and again to spread the gospel of hate, abuse, and genocide. But what if it's not the only monster out there? What if there's something worse? From Dave Brockie, the twisted genius behind GWAR, comes a novel about the darkest days of the twentieth century.

"Highways to Hell" Bryan Smith - The road to hell is paved with angels and demons. Brain worms and dead prostitutes. Serial killers and frustrated writers. Zombies and Rock 'n Roll. And once you start down this path, there is no going back. Collecting thirteen tales of shock and terror from Bryan Smith, Highways to Hell is a non-stop road-trip of cruelty, pain, and death. Grab a seat, Smith has such sights to show you.

"Apeshit" Carlton Mellick III - Friday the 13th meets Visitor Q. Six hipster teens go to a cabin in the woods inhabited by a deformed killer. An incredibly fucked-up parody of B-horror movies with a bizarro slant
"The new gold standard in unstoppable fetus-fucking kill-freakomania . . . Genuine all-meat hardcore horror meets unadulterated Bizarro brainwarp strangeness. The results are beyond jaw-dropping, and fill me with pure, unforgivable joy." - John Skipp

AVAILABLE FROM AMAZON.COM